"You look like ... out of bed," O...

Stevie froze at the i...
bed...Owen Dasher half-naked amidst tangled
sheets, extending a hand to reel her back in.
Heat suffused her cheeks.

"No...I just need to get dressed." She pulled the
skimpy robe tighter around her.

"I see." But his eyes were glued on her hair now.

"Is there a reason you're staring?"

"No...it's just that—" He moved closer, winding
a few tendrils around his fingers.

Stevie held her breath. Her breasts rose and fell
against the cool silk, her nipples peaking in the
chilly room. She knew he wanted to kiss her,
wanted to slip his hands inside her robe.

But instead he said, "It's very strange. Your hair
seems to be, uh, bent...."

Bent? Batting his hand away, she glanced in the
nearby mirror. *Oh, hell.*

Just when Stevie thought she was operating
with confidence and pizzazz, he pointed out she
had *Hee Haw* hair. And she was back to square
one.

She was past that stage, wasn't she? *Stephanie
no more!*

With a determined air, Stevie turned to Owen
and fluffed her hair. "Let me tell you how much
fun it is being...blissfully single."

Dear Reader,

There's just something about Christmas. When the snow starts to fall, when you start to hear the carols and see the lights and the trees…and in Chicago, when the Marshall Field's department store unveils its magical windows, there's romance in the air right along with the snowflakes.

I hope you'll enjoy my look at life and love in Chicago during the holidays as much as I enjoyed dreaming it up. I admit it—I was totally smitten with the idea of an irresistible force like Stevie Bliss, author of a sizzling book about using men for a romp or two while never giving your heart, smacking right up against an immovable object like Owen Dasher, a reporter who thinks she's a total hottie *and* a total fake. Any other time of the year, Stevie might have been able to resist Owen's devastating charms, to stay true to her "Blissfully Single" principles. But there's just something about Christmas….

I hope you'll pull up your comfiest chair, sit back with a cup of cocoa and enjoy this naughty little ride through the holidays!

Merry Christmas!

Julie Kistler

Books by Julie Kistler

HARLEQUIN TEMPTATION
808—JUST A LITTLE FLING

HARLEQUIN DUETS
19—CALLING MR. RIGHT
30—IN BED WITH THE WILD ONE
73—STAND-IN BRIDE
    THE SISTER SWITCH

More Naughty Than Nice

Julie Kistler

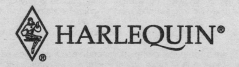

TORONTO • NEW YORK • LONDON
AMSTERDAM • PARIS • SYDNEY • HAMBURG
STOCKHOLM • ATHENS • TOKYO • MILAN • MADRID
PRAGUE • WARSAW • BUDAPEST • AUCKLAND

Dedicated to Scott,
my best Christmas present ever.

ISBN 0-373-69107-6

MORE NAUGHTY THAN NICE

_____Prologue_____

ONE WEEK BEFORE CHRISTMAS. Santa on his way. And Stephanie Blanton already knew what she was going to find in her stocking. A big, fat nothing.

"Gonna find out who's naughty and nice. Yeah, right," she said in an aggrieved tone. "I have always been so nice. And what did it get me?"

No promotion. Not even a hint of a boyfriend or husband with whom to spend the holidays. Sitting in a crummy, noisy, smoke-filled bar a lousy week before Christmas. And if all that weren't bad enough, there were these nasty red and green lights dangling over the table, giving her a terrible headache.

"It's all about expectations," her best friend Anna put in. "We expect too much from men."

Stephanie nodded, doing her best to look wise, which wasn't easy when she'd just slurped down three or four big ol' cosmopolitans. They were cheery and red, and she and Anna had ordered them to feel more Christmasy. Maybe if their drinks had been carried in by a gorgeous man wearing nothing but a sprig of mistletoe. Maybe _then_ she'd feel more festive.

Or maybe not.

"Men," she muttered. "Who needs 'em?"

"Y'see, Steph, when Findlay called you into his office, you thought he would ask you to the Christmas party." Anna hiccuped loudly, but it didn't stop her lecture. "And that's where you went wrong. Because guys like Mr. Findlay don't ask out girls like us. We're too boring, too dull, too nicey-nicey, too—"

"No, no. That's not right." Stephanie sat up straighter on her bar stool, almost falling off but catching herself just in time.

"Which part?"

"I didn't expect Findlay to ask me to the party." She shook her head to clear away the cosmopolitan fog. *Concentrate, Stephanie.* "Okay, Anna, I know you were angling for a date to the office party. But *I* never..."

Anna sent her a cynical look.

"Okay, so maybe, *maybe* I had a tiny, little, baby-size *kernel* of hope that Findlay would ask me," she said, waving a hand, trying to forget the whole misty fantasy she'd spun for herself, all about gorgeous Mr. Findlay, who everyone knew was being promoted out of the cosmetics group, which meant he would no longer be her direct supervisor and therefore could ask her out with carefree abandon.

And what better time than Christmas? Mistletoe, snowflakes, picking out a tree together, eggnog by candlelight...

It just begged for a relationship. Somehow, in her heart of hearts, she had clung to this myth, this fairy tale, that the reason her boss was calling her into his office was to ask her to accompany him not just to the office party, but home next week to meet Mom and Pop Findlay for Christmas dinner. Something right out of *It's a Wonderful Life.*

But the fantasy was gone. Banished. No more. Shaking her head, she finished, "I knew that was way out of the realm of possibility. What I expected—"

"Wait, wait, I know!" Her friend's eyes widened

and she actually giggled, which was not something Anna did very often. "You thought he would knock everything off his desk and then make mad, passionate love to you right then and there, on his desk."

That sobered her up. "On his desk? Eeeeuww."

"That's not it, huh?"

"No way. I have a little more self-respect than that." Stephanie tightened the holly-flecked scrunchie on her plain brown ponytail, forcing herself to return to her senses. It wasn't hot sex she'd wanted from Mr. Findlay. No, it was love and affection and companionship, someone to look at her and think she was special and beautiful, worthy of spending his holidays with. All the things that now felt shabby and stupid. Thank goodness she'd never said any of it out loud. Then she might have to jump off a bridge. This way she just had to drown herself in cosmopolitans.

"What I expected," she explained, "was for him to offer me the promotion to head of the cosmetics group. Because I deserve it. I know it and *he* knows it."

"I know it, too," Anna offered loyally.

Stephanie shook her head. "But, hon, if it wasn't going to be me, it should've been you. You deserve it, too. I'm pretty good when it comes to having a finger on the pulse of our demographic. You, you're even better."

"Maybe. But you do a better presentation. Together we're unbeatable."

"Except for the fact that we've been beaten. By Missy, of all people. *Missy.*" Her voice filled with contempt as she went on, "At our last meeting for the Glam line, Missy actually proposed strawberry as a flavor for lip gloss. Like strawberry hasn't been overdone to death. Like strawberry didn't score in the low twenties with the focus group. Strawberry! It would be funny if it weren't so sad. You'd think we were marketing to six-year-olds. When he told me he was giving her the promotion, my jaw just dropped. I told him about the strawberry fiasco. And he didn't even care."

"That's the whole reason he likes her," Anna argued. "Think about it. She's stupid enough that she will never threaten *his* job."

Stephanie shook her head. "Nope. It's that he wants to boink her."

"Findlay? He would never do that."

"Blond, boobs, boinkability. The whole package," she said gloomily. "It's so unfair."

"I still don't think he would do that," Anna persisted.

"Oh, I don't think he would, either. But he wants to. As long as he *wants* her but doesn't have her, he'll keep her around." Staring into space, she kept a firm grip as she sloshed her wide martini glass back and forth. "See, that's our problem, Anna. No one wants to boink us. What's wrong with them, anyway? We're perfectly boinkable."

"Perfectly," Anna agreed.

"Men are such dolts."

"Totally. Dolt-o-rama."

"And I just don't get why a man like Mr. Findlay, who actually has a brain, would be thinking with his..." She trailed off. It was the curse of being a nice girl. She didn't use words like that in public, even under the influence of alcohol. Missy did, of course. *Missy.* It was just pathetic. "I still can't believe he gave her my promotion. Do you know what he said to me?

He said, 'If you want promotions, you need goals, Stephanie. A five-year plan. Marriage—that's your five-year plan, isn't it? Ha ha.' It's insulting."

"But you're as into your career as anyone. Why would he say that?"

She shrugged. "Because I don't push myself forward, waving my hand, going, *me, me, me!* I don't demand promotions or raises or perks or...anything." Exasperated, she added, "We're the same, Anna, you and me. We're not flashy. We're more in the background. And what's wrong with being in the background? What's wrong with being support staff instead of stars?"

"You're expendable," Anna said flatly. "Not only do you not get promoted, you get fired."

"Oh, Anna, I'm so sorry!" Stephanie said quickly. She couldn't believe she'd been rattling on about her stupid nonpromotion when Anna had it a lot worse. "What they did is so unfair. Goons like Missy make bad choices, the company bleeds accounts right and left, and you get laid off. It makes me want to quit, too."

"It's depressing. Especially at Christmas. I don't mind leaving so much—it's always bothered me that I didn't feel really respected, you know? But still...a job's a job."

Stephanie leaned closer, trying to exude sympathy. "You'll find something else in the New Year. You're too good!"

"I don't care about getting laid off. I'd have to leave, anyway, after what happened today. It was so humiliating." Anna exhaled a long breath. "I made a fool of myself over Fred in Accounting."

"Well, I know you made him a turkey for Thanksgiving, but what's wrong with that?"

But Anna wasn't listening. Staring into the depths of her drink, she muttered, "It was after they sent out the layoff e-mails. I was cleaning out my desk, and Fred stopped by. And suddenly I'm thinking, well, okay, I got laid off, but I wasn't that crazy about working here, anyway, and this could brighten things up. Balance things out, you know? So I'm sitting there, grinning up at him like a goon, with my chubby little fingers crossed. *Is he going to ask me? Is he going to ask me? Oh, goodie. He's opening with the Christmas party. That must mean he's going to ask me!*"

Stephanie leaned in. "So what did he say?"

"He asked me whether I knew any cute girls I could fix him up with at the last minute because he was desperate to have a date for tonight," Anna said darkly. "Like he never thought, for one second, he could ask *me*. I made him a turkey for Thanksgiving. With trimmings! And yet even when he's dying for a date, I'm not good enough. Like what am I, turkey-girl of the Western Hemisphere?"

"Of course not," Stephanie shot back. "You're adorable. And wonderful. And much too good for that jerk."

"Jerk is right. He probably ran right down the hall and asked Missy."

"*Missy*," Stephanie said with a sneer. She was starting to feel outraged all over again. "It's a joke. We are so much more in tune with the Glam demographic. I mean, you and I, Anna, we know where the 18-to-25-year-old woman eats and drinks, her favorite colors, what CDs and videos she buys, who she wants her hair cut like and what celeb she wants to sleep with and why."

"We've got our demographic cold," Anna said sadly. "And nobody cares."

"*I* care. I care about our demographic. I care about all those poor 18-to-25-year-olds who are going to be pushed into buying the wrong cosmetics because stupid Missy is in charge." Resolute, Stephanie raised her glass. "I promise you this, Anna. I will not let my demographic down. I will do what I can to combat the Missies of this world, so that the 18-to-25-year-olds coming up will not be forced to wear strawberry lip gloss in the pursuit of the Glam lifestyle."

"You go, girl!" Anna stopped. "But how are you going to do that?"

Stephanie thought for a long moment, but nothing came to her. Finally, she set her cocktail glass back down on the table. "I don't know yet."

Narrowing her eyes, Anna chewed on the end of a maraschino cherry stem. "There has to be some way we can use what we know. We've worked so hard."

"Exactly. And I know we can think of something. We're smart, we're committed and we have a lot to say." Warming to her topic, Stephanie declared, "The women of the twenty-first century need to know what we have to tell them."

"Like how to turn the tables." Her friend smiled gleefully. "Like, what are you thinking, girls? You do not need to get hooked up with some loser and let him bring you down."

"Exactly," Stephanie said firmly. "Like you should never sit around waiting for a man to call. Better yet, you should sleep with whoever you want and then not take his calls or return his messages. Better the dumper then the dumpee, you know?"

"This is good, Steph!"

"The women of tomorrow should do what they want, when they want. Forget marriage. Forget all those nasty bonds that only benefit the men." *Marriage—that's your five-year plan, isn't it, Stephanie?* Mr. Findlay's mocking words played back in her mind, spurring her on. "We'll come right out and say, hey, bucko, I want to sleep with you, but you can darn well do your own laundry and pick out your own ties and, and—"

"And make your own Thanksgiving turkey!"

"And trimmings! We should never share our money, our closets or our bathrooms—"

"Oooh. Bathrooms. Excellent one," Anna chimed in. "No fighting over seats up, seats down, which way the toilet paper roll goes, any of that."

"Because we don't need them or any of their baggage!"

Anna's volume rose as she came in with, "You are so right! Not in my bathroom! Not with your baggage! But lots of sex. Everywhere, anywhere, all the time! Sex!"

Stephanie suddenly noticed all the attention they were getting in the crowded bar. Anna went on, blithely indifferent, bouncing on her barstool and slamming a fist into the air, as her voice grew increasingly louder.

"Boink 'em and throw 'em away! Woo-hoo!"

"Anna, maybe you should—"

"No, listen, Steph. We should *so* do this! A new message for a new century. Gloria Steinem meets Britney Spears. Independence. The bad girl. The independent bad girl! It's perfect!"

"Okay, well, let's not run away with ourselves."

"No, no, you don't see." Anna leaned closer. "I don't have a job, and you'll be working for Missy. They don't respect either of us, and we don't have to put up with that. So you're going to go back to work on the Monday after New Year's and tell Findlay that you quit."

"I am?"

"Yes, you are. And then we'll have the time. We already have the brains. And we have you."

"Me?" Stephanie asked dimly. "What does that mean?"

"Well, we can't go revolutionizing women without a spokesmodel." Anna crossed her arms over her chest. "Face it. No matter what we do to me, I'm still going to be too short and too square. But you... You've got real possibilities. You could be really hot if we put some Tae Bo and a few Glam products where our mouth is. Besides, you're great at presentations, remember? You pitch like nobody else. This is like one big pitch."

"But, Anna..." Stephanie peered at her friend. "How did we get from 'boink 'em and dump 'em' to me being a spokesmodel? I am *so* not the type. I'm way too nice!"

"But that's just it. Inside, I think there is definitely a naughty girl itching to get out."

"Out of *me*?"

"You bet! Babe, you and me, we know women ages 18 to 25 like the back of our hand," Anna argued. "We know exactly who they want to be. So we provide the who. You! I do the marketing, you write the results, you *live* the results. This is so perfect."

"Are you talking a how-to?" Stephanie asked. "Or something more like a like a video or a magazine?"

"We'll figure that out later. Put some focus groups together and see what plays the best."

"But what's our message?"

"We've already got it. The independent bad girl. Spike your stiletto heel through his heart!"

"That's a tad violent, isn't it?"

"Okay, then—sassy sisters doing it for themselves. Guys are for fun, but not for forever." Anna beamed with satisfaction. "We make up for every Fred in Accounting, for every Mr. Findlay who ever picked a bimbo over the smart girl. We show them all who knows what about marketing. And our demographic eats it up with a spoon."

Stephanie blinked. She couldn't quite believe it, but this all made sense. Cold, hard, perfect sense.

"So?" Anna prompted, raising her cosmopolitan in a half toast. "Do we show them what we're made of?"

Sassy sisters doing it for themselves. She *loved* it! She could already see the marketing plan, the product tie-ins, the PR possibilities dancing before her eyes.

No more Ms. Nice Girl... Letting out the naughty girl inside... Stephanie smiled with grim satisfaction as she lifted her own glass. "Let's do it, Anna. Let's show the world."

1

A few days before Thanksgiving, three years later

"STEVIE, DO YOU THINK we should ice down your nipples before you go out?"

Stevie Bliss, aka Stephanie Blanton, author of the fabulously successful new book, *Blissfully Single*, whipped around so fast she almost knocked her assistant over. "Anna, are you nuts?" she whispered. "Ice down my...? You're kidding, right?"

"Of course I'm not kidding." Anna fixed her with a stubborn stare. "Nipples happen to be big right now. Our focus group went off the charts when they saw video of J. Lo at the—"

"I'm not doing it," Stevie interrupted. "Besides, I'm wearing a jacket. Nobody would see them, anyway."

"Are you sure?" Anna persisted. "We've gotten as much play as we're going to get off the rest of our outthere elements. Maybe one more is just what we need for a new round of press. We're coming up on the biggest shopping day of the year. We've got to keep you in the public eye."

Stevie almost smacked her. Anna was her best friend, her confidante and her partner in this crazy plot to put them and *Blissfully Single* on the map, but sometimes she really went too far.

"I've done everything you've asked, Anna, includ-

ing the no underwear thing, which I personally think
is ridiculous—"

"It killed on the surveys and you know it," Anna
returned. She began to tick items off on her fingers.
"For our last element, we gave them a choice of tattoo,
various piercings, magenta or blue hair, exposed mid-
riff, exposed thong and even carrying a snake. Nothing scored like going commando."

"I know, I know."

"It makes you naughty, outrageous, but not too far
over the line. And it gives us an advantage over most
men, who are so distracted by what may be going on
under there that they forget to feel threatened by the
message."

"I know, I know."

Sounding just a tad testy, Anna said, "I don't make
this stuff up, Stevie. It's all in the hard data."

"And I have done everything so far that skewed
right with that data," Stevie explained patiently. "But
the whole thing, the whole Stevie Bliss persona, it's set
now. Set. In stone. Or at least in leather."

She took a deep breath, looking down at the slick
black leather miniskirt and zip jacket, both scandal-
ously expensive, the deeply plunging neckline on the
silk camisole underneath, the knee-high boots with
three-inch heels... She had never imagined herself
strutting around in an outfit like this. And whether
you called it a hottie or a 'ho, it certainly made an impact.

She'd tried hard to own this new brazen person she
had become. Day in and day out, she continued to try.
And she was doing pretty well, if she did say so herself. For the past month, ever since they'd launched
this leg of the official media tour for *Blissfully Single*,

she and Anna and their PR machine had been blitzing the East Coast markets. Everyone from Letterman to Liz Smith had bought into Stevie Bliss, champion of the single, sexy, independent woman, confident in her own sizzling womanhood.

And now they'd brought their act to Chicago for the holidays. They had a month of appearances and signings designed to saturate the Midwest from their base in the Windy City, where there was fabulous shopping and exactly the right demographic of shoppers.

Meanwhile, every piece of her persona, from the streaks in her hair to the shape of her "smart girl" glasses and the precise amount of cleavage she showed, had been carefully selected, based on hours of marketing research. She looked terrific. She didn't need iced nipples to sell this package.

"But Stevie—"

She held up a hand. "Anna, give it up."

The bookstore manager peeked around the corner into the office, cutting off further discussion. "Ms. Bliss? We have everything set up. Are you ready?"

Stevie raised her chin. "Absolutely," she said, with the lazy drawl that was her trademark. Soft and sexy, with a hint of a growl, this was the voice that played best with her public.

From recent experience, Stevie knew she would be fine as long as she stuck with the program and played the role to the hilt, safe behind the disguise. Reminding herself—as some psychological consultant or other had recommended—that she was a cool jungle cat, she strode out behind the man from the bookstore, sliding carefully and yet easily into the chair next to the podium, perched at the front of her seat with her knees down so as not to show off anything she didn't want to. Instead, she offered a polished smile and more than a hint of décolletage to the eager fans in the front row.

I'm a tiger, they're hyenas, and I will eat them all alive.

Whoa. They were really crammed in here today, weren't they? Anna would be pleased—every seat was filled, with more fans standing around the sides and in the back, all clutching hardcover copies of *Blissfully Single.* There were also two TV cameras shooting across the crowd from different sides, but it didn't faze her. Stations frequently sent someone out to her appearances to get some footage for the evening news, maybe collect a sound bite or two. As constructed, the Stevie Bliss persona was telegenic, so getting on camera was the whole idea.

On the sides, Stevie could see bookstore clerks trying to shove racks and shelves farther back to accommodate extra people. Such a big crowd. Butterflies flickered in her stomach, and she really had to clamp down. *You're a tiger, damn it!*

The store manager was halfway through his introduction, playing to the closer camera as he told the assembled folks how lucky they were to get to see Stevie Bliss, author extraordinaire, up close and personal, how much her book had meant to so many, and on and on. Stevie tuned out, trying to judge the people in the crowd. Would they be receptive? Or would they throw tomatoes, with the TV cameras catching every splash?

The stony faces over on the left side—the ones near the baby carriage—looked like protesters for sure. Moms on parade, no doubt, who felt the need to fight for the sanctity of marriage. She'd seen their ilk before.

Ditto the group of men nearer the back, shuffling as they stood. Although most of her fans were female, she tended to get a good number of men, too, the kind who wanted to meet the daring woman who boasted short skirts and no panties, who made no bones about the fact that she slept with whoever she liked, had no interest in anything permanent, and would only stay with a man for one month, tops. For them, it was like an open invitation. Meet the hottie! Get her to give *you* a month!

It wasn't going to happen—her scandalous reputation was all smoke and no fire—but she wasn't going to tell them that.

For others, and these grumpy guys looked like they fell squarely into the "other" category, it was more of a war. A bit older, a lot more insecure as they looked ahead to hair implants and Viagra, they hated the idea that a woman would claim the upper hand when it came to sex. They showed up to boo on behalf of their beleaguered gender.

Stevie held her head high. Mentally, she had classified and discarded them. Hadn't she had hours of training on how to deflect hard questions? She could handle a few measly hecklers. Besides, they provided good publicity, even if they did give her headaches. *Tiger, tiger,* she repeated under her breath, smiling brightly as she watched one of the TV guys shift for a different view. But when he moved to the side, her eyes were drawn to the man behind him, someone who had been hidden until now.

Hold on. Who was *he?* He didn't fit the profile of either the wannabe wolf or the macho man. Chewing her lip, she ticked off the important details, trying to get a handle on Mr. Way Cute. Sitting by himself, dark hair, piercing gaze, very good-looking, cool and removed, carrying a small notebook flipped open to the first page....

Reporter, she decided. If there was such a thing as a really hot reporter who looked like George Clooney's younger brother. Did reporters come like that? She'd been interviewed quite a few times, but never by anyone who looked like this one.

The mystery man paid no attention to the bookstore manager, who was still up at the podium, droning on through that endless introduction. Instead, he stared right through her. His gaze was frank, speculative, insolent, raking over her, judging her. He sat back in his chair, putting his pen aside. The challenge was palpable, crackling in the air between them. *I don't think you're so special. You're going to have to prove it, baby. Every word.*

She swallowed. Okay, well, if he was going to be that way, she would just have to turn up her sex appeal another notch, past "ensnare" and right up to "torture." She could do that. Right?

She looked at him. He looked at her. He narrowed that sharp gaze. And suddenly she felt a lot less like a tiger and a lot more like a hyena.

Breaking first, Stevie scooted to the side and sent a frantic glance Anna's way, signaling that she needed help. Anna was excellent when it came to picking up on the "panic" vibe, and she rushed over, bending in. "What?" she whispered.

"Back row," Stevie murmured. "Reporter. Who is he?"

"Oh." Anna relaxed. "Owen Dasher, a columnist from the *Chicago Chronicle*. It's the third-rated paper in town. But he's a real up-and-comer."

"I sense a certain..." She licked her lip. "Hostility."

Anna spared him a quick glance. "I don't think he looks hostile."

"Very Cary Grant in *Notorious*. He needs Ingrid Bergman to sleep with Claude Rains as part of this spy thing, but then when she does, well, he thinks she's a 'ho. Very hostile."

Anna was steeled and ready to jump before Stevie got to the end of her thought. "What have I told you about the old movie thing? I know it's a habit, but it's not sexy. It makes you sound more like a geek on the trivia bowl team."

They'd been through this a million times. Could she help it if she *had* once been a geek on the high school trivia bowl team? And she adored old movies. The flickering black-and-white images on the classic film channels had everything the real world did not.

Still, she knew Anna was right. Old movies might fit Stephanie Blanton, but not Stevie Bliss. And a hefty percentage of their target demographic hadn't seen anything made before *Titanic*.

"Okay, okay. Nix on the movies. Back to the reporter." She ventured a glance his direction. Cary Grant? Ha! Okay, so he had the dark hair, a penetrating gaze, a classic jawline, even a certain elegance in the way he held himself. But he was no Cary Grant. She was sure of that. Quickly skipping back to Anna, she asked, "What do you think he wants?"

"A column, obviously," Anna said impatiently. "Maybe if you really make an impression, he'll do more than one. I told you about him. The *Tribune* and the *Sun-Times* dissed us, but the *Chronicle* sent him. I looked up some of his columns, just to check him out. He's good. Seems to champion causes a lot, although he does some satirical stuff, too. Not exactly who I'd pick to write about you, but he has a following. He may have an agenda, I don't know. And I don't really care." She smiled. "I have no doubt you can turn him around."

"Right." Owen Dasher of the *Chronicle*, huh? She frowned.

"Don't frown. And quit chewing off your lipstick. Smile," Anna ordered. "Look happy and in charge."

"Yeah, yeah."

"Stevie? Uh, Ms. Bliss?"

She glanced over at the bookstore manager, who was speaking in a stage whisper and beckoning with one hand. "Yes?"

"I'm done with my... I mean, you're on. Now."

"Oh." Damn it, anyway. All caught up in the irritating man in the back row, she'd missed her cue. And now she felt flustered and off balance. *You're a tiger and they're hyenas,* she reminded herself quickly as she swept up to the podium, facing down her audience. She focused on a smiling young woman in the front row, exactly the right age and attitude to be receptive.

But it was that damn man in the back row she was thinking about. She was going to have to be at the top of her game to sell her message with him staring at her.

You're Stevie Bliss, she told herself. *You can do it.*

Deliberately, she swung her head around, she found him in the crowd, and she began to speak right to him.

"Definitely single," she purred. "And totally satisfied. Let me tell you all about it."

OWEN DASHER felt himself fall neatly into the palm of her hot little hand.

And how exactly had she done that? He'd come prepared to be unimpressed. Bored, cynical, a little annoyed his editor had made him do this, he'd sat there as the crowd filled in, making a quick first draft of the column he intended to write.

Yet another attempt to hijack women's brains and send them to Never Never Land, he scribbled into his notebook. Stevie Bliss—who is as fake as her Power-puff name—takes up where the Spice Girls and Ally McBeal thankfully left off....

He smiled. An excellent turn of phrase. That one just might make the final cut and end up in his column.

He might've thought he was being unfair, but he couldn't miss the fact that there were other people here who didn't care for her, either, what with the guy standing behind him who kept muttering, "Crazy broad," and the ladies clustered around the baby carriage on the other side, all prim and proper in their disapproval. Good. He was looking forward to some fireworks.

And then she was late. As the bookstore got fuller and fuller, Owen grew more annoyed. It didn't help that he didn't want to be there in the first place, pretending he cared about the *Blissfully Single* crowd. He'd read the book. He knew how slick, shallow and maybe even dangerous her message was.

All that stuff about women who refused to get married and used men as sex objects struck him as pretty ridiculous. He'd had plenty of one-nighters in his twenty-nine years on the planet, and he'd learned from hard experience that being involved with someone purely for the sex always turned out ugly. He didn't think there had to be love involved, necessarily, but he didn't think you should be sleeping with someone if you couldn't bear to wake up with them, either. Okay, so he was opinionated. He was a columnist. It came with the territory.

As he'd waited, he'd mused on why she came up with this stuff. What had made Stevie Bliss so cynical about love and relationships?

His first thought was that she must be some dried-up crone who couldn't get a guy in the first place. He checked her picture. No dried-up crone there. But, hey, digital touch-ups were amazing. So who knew?

Or maybe she was no more than another fast-buck artist, mouthing whatever phony baloney self-help platitudes she thought were most likely to net her some easy cash. The crude, rude flavor of the month, clad in leather, sporting no undies just to get some attention.

As he was mulling the question one more time, the real Stevie Bliss walked out. No, she *sauntered* out, all long legs and saucy attitude. He noted the streaked blond hair, cut kind of wispy and choppy on the ends where it brushed her shoulders, the striking blue eyes behind snappy little tortoiseshell glasses, the creamy, pale skin curving down into that daring camisole, the skirt that was barely long enough to cover her assets... Wow.

If this was a dried-up crone, he was Methuselah. And far from vulgar, she seemed to have found the place where sex met class and lived happily ever after.

Letting his gaze linger on her spectacular legs, he wondered whether those boots were made for walking. And on whom. He had to admit it. She was hot.

He could see she was impatient as the introduction limped on, as her eyes scanned the room, taking the measure of the crowd, checking for pockets of negativity she might have to combat later. Smart girl.

And then her electric gaze hit him. Pow. One glance from media creation Stevie Bliss and he was sautéed in his seat. Where in the hell did that come from?

At first he wondered if this smoky glance thing was some tactic she tried on all the men in her audience. But no, she seemed to be as thunderstruck as he was. And she was gazing directly at him, no one else.

He steeled himself against his own overheated reaction. Owen Dasher was no neophyte when it came to dazzling women, after all. He'd interviewed a heap of stars as they hit Chicago to promote their movies, and if Julia Roberts couldn't reduce him to a pile of goo, there was no way he was going to melt after one glance from Stevie Bliss.

So they did a little visual tango, eye to eye, with him hanging on to a sense of journalistic detachment by his fingernails. *She's shallow and plastic and this is all a scam*, he reminded himself. And he was pleased—no, relieved—when she broke first to talk to one of her handlers. She seemed rattled, and he enjoyed that, too.

Relaxing for the first time since their gazes intersected, he managed to collect himself, taking himself sternly to task for losing it like that. But, yeah, he could handle her. He'd just proved that. She'd looked away first, hadn't she?

Then she sidled up to the podium to begin her speech, and he felt his palms start to sweat. Okay, so her long, lovely legs and those wicked boots were hidden behind the podium. That helped. But the rest of her, still on display, was a lot to deal with. A lot of warm, delicious woman. His fingers began to clench and unclench, and he realized he hadn't taken a single note. *Hell.*

As she spoke, purring about sassy sisters who knew their personal value and took no prisoners, she was staring right at him, giving him the full benefit of this little performance. Although his brain couldn't seem to process a word she was saying, he was actually starting to believe her.

"I love men," she confided, in a naughty tone of voice that sent sparks of heat licking up from the bottom of his spine. He stretched his legs, pretending to be bored, adjusting his position. Still burning.

"People call me a man-hater," she continued, lifting a dismissive hand in the air. "Isn't that silly? It couldn't be farther from the truth. I love men. I mean, I *love* them."

As she drew out the word "love" to make her implication clear, she was met by a flurry of giggles, and she turned her focus to the gaggle of teens in the front row, the ones doing the giggling. Which distracted her from keeping him pinned to his seat. *Thank God.*

"And why not? Men have been taking the cake and eating it, too, forever. Now it's time for *my* cake." Her smile widened, and she had a mischievous gleam in her eyes that left no doubt what she was really talking about. Sex. "Maybe with whipped cream and a cherry on top."

Whipped cream? And a cherry on top? On top of what? Or whom? Owen groaned, slipping deeper into the fantasy.

And then Stevie licked her lip. That pretty pink little tongue flicked over her top lip, for only a second. He was a goner.

Oh, man. This was bad. Very bad.

As she moved away from whipped cream, talking instead about empowerment and freedom, about making good choices and having no fear, he could feel the crowd moving with her. He could feel *himself* moving with her. He wanted to believe her. He wanted to stand up and shout, "Yes! Yes!" along with the rest of the converts.

Hell, he wanted to throw her on the floor and make love to her until *she* screamed, "Yes! Yes!"

Time to get a grip.

Reining himself in with fierce control, Owen glared at her. She was manipulating everyone in this room, and he was not going to be part of it.

Finally it was time for questions. He looked to the groups of dissenters he'd identified earlier. Surely they could bring her down a peg or two. *Go to it, guys! Dent that sex kitten veneer.*

"Miss Bliss," a rather stodgy-looking woman called out, raising her hand, which was weighted down by a huge diamond and a thick wedding ring. Several other women rose behind her, and they lifted neatly printed signs into the air. *Mom, Marriage and Apple Pie* read one, while another went with *Bliss is a Big Liar!*

"I prefer Ms.," Stevie Bliss responded quickly. "Or you can just call me Stevie. Would you prefer that?"

"No. Yes. I mean, *no.*" The lady with the question looked ready to burst a blood vessel. "I do not want to call you anything. Our group, the Righteous Moms Brigade, believes that marriage and motherhood should be respected and commended, not spit upon, as you seem to do, and we would like to say that your book is just hateful—"

"Don't you just love what she said about marriage and motherhood?" Stevie cut in. "Isn't that wonderful? Respected and commended. You are so right. Because if it weren't for women like you, who are on the frontlines of the marriage wars, the rest of us, the ones who are totally unsuited for that life, might have to sub in. So let's give the Righteous Moms a hand, shall we? We love you, Righteous Moms!"

As the other women present dutifully applauded, Stevie added, "I hope everyone will read chapter five of *Blissfully Single,* where I talk about how you decide what's right for you. It's not whether you choose to be married or single that counts. It's about having the choice, about being smart and not being afraid to go it alone if that's what really suits you."

And with that, she dismissed the Righteous Moms from her radar and moved on. They were still sputtering over there, but she had pretty much stripped them of their weapons by agreeing with them. Besides, she was in charge of the questions, and she wouldn't call on any more of them.

The next set of questions was less contentious, all about what makeup she used and what designer she was wearing, before three or four guys in a row asked if they could sign up for a month of her time. "A month, a week, whatever," one of them offered breathlessly. He was young and didn't seem very bright, with his backward baseball cap and goofy grin, but he certainly didn't look like he was insane or anything. "Hey, Stevie, I'll take an hour if that's all ya got. Ten minutes. Whatever."

He couldn't believe it when Stevie Bliss actually

grinned back at the kid. "Aren't you adorable?" she declared. "I'm in the market, too. My December calendar has plenty of spots. So you just get in line, and bring ID, please, so we can make sure you're old enough, and then I will definitely put you on my list of contenders."

Owen rolled his eyes at the level of bull being shoveled here. Who in his right mind would sign up to march in Stevie Bliss's never-ending parade of boy toys?

Finally, a cranky gent from the back of the room pushed forward far enough to get to talk. He had a buzz cut, a Chicago Bears jacket and a sour look on his face, all of which tended to suggest he wasn't a Bliss fan. Yet Stevie actually called on him.

"Yes? You, sir."

"My name is Joe Ramsey, and I'm the president of the Swingin' He-Men, Chicago chapter."

"How lovely for you, I'm sure," she said sweetly.

"Well, thanks." He swaggered a little, building up steam as he unfolded a piece of paper and read from it. "So, anyway, we want to know who you think you are, emasculating the male half of the society with your wanting to take our place as the predators and the hunters and all." He glanced up expectantly. "Well?"

"Mr. He-Man, you hunt and predate all you want." She lifted her slender shoulders in a shrug. "I don't mind a bit."

"But what about you getting in the way and telling women they get to dump us whenever they feel like it? That they shouldn't do our laundry or make our food or any of the other stuff women are supposed to do. That's just wrong!"

"I agree with you, Joe. Women being forced to do your laundry or make your food, that's just wrong. Isn't it nice we can agree on something?" She smiled and turned away from him before he sorted out exactly what she'd said to him, as she pretended to catch sight of the clock. "Oh, dear," she said regretfully. "I'm afraid our time is up. Thank you so much, everyone, for coming out to see me today. I'll be happy to sign your books if you'd like to line up."

Which they did, like lambs to the slaughter. There was even a traitor from the Swingin' He-Men who came tramping into the line with his book under his arm, blushing and looking sheepish.

Owen was grudgingly impressed. Two protesters turned back without a hint of a dustup. No fistfights, not even a raised voice. Too bad.

"Mr. Dasher?" It was the handler, the one he'd seen chatting with Stevie before her talk. Where Stevie wore leather and displayed all the right skin on her long, lithe frame, this short, somewhat stout lady was buttoned into a nondescript brown wool suit with a plain white blouse. Big-boned and broad-shouldered, with a square jaw and a no-nonsense expression, she looked more like a Righteous Mom than someone who'd be riding the *Blissfully Single* train.

"I'm Owen Dasher," he said. "You are...?"

"Anna, Stevie's assistant." She fixed him with a level gaze. "Sorry about the delay. There's such a long line for autographs, and she may be a while. So if you wanted to—"

"Leave?" he asked with a shade of annoyance. Stevie Bliss got him all whipped into a frenzy by sending him lascivious glances and licking her lips and talking about whipped cream, and now she was going to leave him hanging? "What, is she afraid of this interview? You can tell her not to worry. I don't bite."

In a testier tone, she said, "You heard her speak. Do you really think she's afraid of an interview? I think she's looking forward to meeting you, as a matter of fact. She just wondered if you might prefer to go get a latte at the coffee bar while you wait."

"Oh." He stuck his notebook in the pocket of his coat, made a move to leave and then stayed where he was. Where was the coffee bar, anyway? And why would anyone think he was a latte kind of guy? Should he be insulted? "Look, that's fine. Whatever. I'll be at the coffee bar."

"Mr. Dasher?"

He glanced back, noting that Anna looked more smug now than awkward. "Yes?"

"I thought you might want to know. Stevie..." Her words trailed off as she laughed out loud. "You should be prepared. She *does* bite."

2

"Woo-hoo!" Stevie was so excited that she chugged water down too fast and spilled some on her Prada leather jacket. "I was good, wasn't I?" she asked Anna. "I mean, I was *on* today. I had 'em cold. I cooked! I *ruled!*"

"You ruled," Anna agreed. "There was a big crowd, and we sold a ton of books."

"I was in a groove." She swiveled in her chair, too hyped up to sit still. "At first that reporter guy kind of threw me, but then I took it as a challenge. Did you see how cute he was? I mean, awfully cute. Very, very cute. Men like him, all cool and superior and gorgeous and way too sure of themselves, they are exactly why we started this. And today, I was a tiger and he was a hyena and it felt *good*. Mr. Way Cute, and I reeled him in. By the end, he practically had a hook in his mouth."

"I'm glad you enjoyed it," Anna said dryly. "Better get a move on. He's waiting in the coffee bar."

She rolled her eyes. "I know, I know. I'll be there in a sec. I was enjoying the moment, that's all."

"Yeah, well, hooked or not, he seemed kind of ticked off. I wouldn't want to push him." Frowning, Anna blotted the wet spot on Stevie's jacket with a tissue. "I don't know what burr he's got under his saddle, but there's something."

Stevie leaned forward, more alert now. "You think he's planning to trash me?"

Anna shrugged. "Dunno. It doesn't really matter. Trash or flash, it's still publicity. As long as he writes a column, that's all I care. Or maybe if you get under his skin enough, he'll come across with two or three columns. And then we get a slew of letters to the editor, pro and con, and the other papers will tune in to the controversy and they'll run features and pictures, too." She took Stevie by the hand and pulled her out of her chair, propelling her toward the door and her duty. "The shopping season is just getting started. If we play our cards right, there will be moms and daughters and sisters and cousins and friends, all dying to buy copies of *Blissfully Single* for each other. Believe me, we need the press. So get to work. Get under his skin."

Stevie considered. "Under his skin... Would that be irritated or turned on?"

"I don't know." Anna smiled, holding open the door as Stevie reluctantly ducked through. "Whatever works. Seems like you made a pretty good start. So keep it up."

"Hmm..."

As Anna lagged behind, looking for a lost press kit with some updated stats she wanted to give to the reporter, Stevie put her glasses back on and shook her head so her hair would fall into just the right tousled disarray. She threw back her shoulders and lengthened her stride.

She wasn't afraid of one silly reporter. Not in the least. So why was her heart pounding like a runaway bongo drum as she swept into the bookstore's coffee bar?

There he was, with his dark hair carelessly shoved off his forehead, gnawing on the end of a pen. As he sat there, unaware of her scrutiny, she tried to be clinical and objective. She noted that he was tall, fairly slim and very good-looking, even with that grumpy expression. He was wearing a crisp white dress shirt, open at the neck, with a tailored navy blazer and tan pants. Neat, well-organized, comfortable in his clothes. Nothing so scary about that, was there? Chewing her lip, she wished she could find something about him, some obvious flaw, so that she could dismiss him outright.

Damn him, anyway. At first glance, he looked perfect. Or maybe that was his flaw. Who wanted perfection?

As she strolled over, his green eyes took her measure one more time. She did her best to look careless and at ease as she slipped into the other seat at his small wooden table. For the first time in a long time, she was intensely aware that the curves of her breasts were right there on display, inches from his eyes, that her skirt was very short and tight and... And that she wasn't wearing any panties.

Was she sweating everywhere all at once? Or did it just feel like it?

Hello, Owen Dasher. Hello, Nightmare City.

Oh, come on. He probably hadn't read the book and didn't have a clue about the stupid no-underwear thing. Sure he was getting a good gander at her cleavage, but so what? Lots of women wore low necklines. And he was much too close to look under her skirt.

No squirming, she told herself curtly. *No panicking. And no squirming!*

"Hello," she began, meeting his cool gaze. With her

skirt firmly in place, she pressed her legs together, leaned forward, and extended a hand. "You must be Owen Dasher."

He ignored her hand, preferring to glance down at his notebook. Then he slapped a small tape recorder down on the table between them. "Right. I already know who you are."

Ooooh. Nice voice. Husky, a shade gruff, yet with a certain note of sweetness. It made her feel all melty. Of course, she was already overly warm, so it wasn't that big a leap. But the voice could almost make her forgive the fact that he didn't want to take her hand. Almost.

She pulled herself away from dangerous thoughts and concentrated on How to Manipulate a Conversation 101.

"I certainly hope you know who I am," she returned smoothly. "You were staring a hole in me all the time I was speaking. So, did you like what you saw?"

That got him to look up. Bad move. She found herself momentarily distracted by his eyes. Chilly, yes. But that particular deep shade of green was amazing, particularly accented by his thick, dark lashes. Like a cool dip in a forest glade.

Snap out of it, she ordered herself. Probably colored contacts. Didn't she know herself how easy it was to change your eye color? He probably did it just to bamboozle impressionable interviewees like her.

When he responded, his tone was as cynical as his eyes. "I'm trying to figure out if this *Blissfully Single* stuff is a scam or a joke."

Rule 1: If you don't like the question you're asked, re-

spond with one of your own. "Are those the only two choices?"

"I don't know yet."

"You listened to my speech," she noted. "Or at least you stared at me during my speech. Did that provide any clues?"

"Not really."

"Why? Not paying attention, were we?"

"Oh, I paid attention."

"I thought so." She was kind of enjoying this verbal thrust and parry. As long as she fenced with him, word for word, it kept her mind off her lack of lingerie, the tiny thread of perspiration sliding down between her breasts and the hypnotic look in his beautiful eyes.

He said, "I found out one thing. You're very good at what you do."

Then he edged his heavy wooden chair forward, far enough that if she kicked out her boot an inch or two, she'd get him right in the shin. Which might not be a bad idea. But he'd made his point. His physical presence was strong and intimidating, generating enough body heat to knock her whole chair over. She dug in. She wasn't going anywhere. Although some cold water thrown on her head might've been nice. Better yet, cold water thrown on *his* head.

Instead, she simply said, "Thank you. I'll take that as a compliment."

His jaw clenched. He sounded frustrated when he shot back, "Take it any way you want. I meant that you've obviously practiced delivering your spiel, you make a slick presentation, you sell what you've got to sell and the morons who buy your book get what they deserve."

Stevie lifted an eyebrow. "And you've decided they're morons because you don't like my message, you don't like my fans or because you're threatened by *me*?"

"None of the above."

"Then what? What is your problem, Mr. Dasher?"

"Who said I had a problem?"

She was losing control of this interview, letting him ruffle her feathers. And she had no intention of letting that continue. She was supposed to be getting under *his* skin, not vice versa.

Rule 2: Be calm, but establish who's boss. Draw a line in the sand. Keeping her voice cool and collected, she mused, "I think you should quit playing footsie with me, Mr. Dasher. This is supposed to be an interview, remember? So far you haven't asked any real questions, have you?"

She bent nearer, giving him a steady gaze that she hoped disguised her real feelings. *I am going to smoke you, Mr. Big Shot. You think you can confuse me with how hot you are? You think I don't know you just called my readers morons? You are going* down!

He stared back, enigmatic and annoying.

Rule 3: Put him on the defensive. She struck. "Are you having problems getting your questions together? Don't be afraid. Why, you can ask me anything, and find out every little thing you ever wanted to know about the *Blissfully Single* life, or..." Tipping her head to one side, she offered a superior smile. "Let me guess. You'd rather talk about *you*, right? 'Cause, after all, you're the guy here. You're used to everything revolving around you. Poor little dear. This must be confusing, when you're not the center of attention."

But he didn't take the bait. "I've got questions."

"Fire when ready." *Get that revolver out of the holster, big boy.*

Fast and snappy, he asked, "Where did you get the idea for the book? Bad marriage? Some guy dump you? No date for the prom?"

"Do I look like a woman scorned?"

"I don't know. Do you?"

"No." She leaned in even closer, so that they were knee to knee, eye to eye. And if he wanted to stare right down the front of her camisole, well, that view was available. But he didn't. His eyes stayed on hers. Darn him. She'd been sure she could distract him with some cleavage. Charging ahead, she finished, "I'm perfectly happy in my relationships. Plural. Always have been."

"Ever been married?"

"No."

"Left at the altar?"

"No. How about you?"

He grinned, and it was so swift and genuine, she couldn't breathe for just a second. *He's enjoying this, too. He's as turned on as I am!*

"No and no," he said. "So if you've never done it, what do you have against marriage?"

"If you've never done it, why are you defending it?"

"I'm supposed to ask the questions, and you're supposed to answer. Which you didn't." His voice dropped lower as he repeated, "What *do* you have against marriage?"

Luckily, she had a series of set responses to that particular question—it was the first one everyone always asked—so she could pull another easy answer out of a mental file without thinking about his smile, his even white teeth, his perfectly formed lips....

I want you to kiss me with those lips. Now. Often. Starting with now.

On automatic pilot, she murmured, "Marriage is a lovely institution. But I don't want to live in an institution."

"I've heard that before," he breathed, and his hand slid onto her knee.

"Doesn't make it any less true," she whispered. Stevie fixed her gaze on his adorable mouth, not even hearing his words.

Who cared? She was stoked up. She was on fire. His fingers crept an inch or two higher, tickling and warming her skin at the same time. The sensation—so small, so inconsequential—was incredible. God, that felt good.

She slipped to the front of her seat, rubbing one boot along his calf. He leaned in, lining up for the kiss she knew was coming. But it didn't. He just sat there, waiting, as the air between them crackled with possibilities.

Feeling very naughty, she licked her bottom lip, watching his eyes as they followed her tongue. Secure in her hot-to-trot persona, she whispered, "So are you going to kiss me or not, Mr. Dasher?"

"Why would I do that, Ms. Bliss?" he asked, in the same soft, dangerous tone she was using.

She kept her boot on his leg. "Why wouldn't you? You know you want to."

"I do?"

"Oh, yeah. You do."

"I don't kiss women I barely know."

"So get to know me." *Fast. And then kiss me.*

As he gazed at her with a definite spark of mischief and heat, she knew she had him right where she wanted him. She was so proud of herself for acting sexy and reckless—right out of the *Blissfully Single* playbook—until she suddenly realized she was making a huge mistake. Playing at reckless was fine. Really *being* reckless was terrible.

As besotted as she was, she still recognized they needed a power shift here. Quickly. Or she'd be in the storage closet making mad, passionate love with Mr. Way Cute before she knew it. She had never done anything that crazy and irresponsible in her entire life, with or without a storage closet and Mr. Way Cute. No matter what she pretended to be, she was not the right sort of person for this full-on assault.

Sliding her foot back to her own side of the table, she decided to say something crude enough to knock him off his game. "If you're trying to play it coy, you don't need to. Anyone who's read my book knows it's not that hard to get into my pants."

"But, Stevie, anyone who's read your book knows you don't wear any."

He'd read the book. He knew.

Panic and excitement trilled deep inside her. His soft breath ruffled her hair as he tilted in near her ear. Down below, his hand flirted under the edge of her leather skirt. *Oh, man.* He'd read the book. He knew!

That was so unfair. She was wet, she was burning up, she wanted him. She closed her eyes and leaned into his fingers, letting him go wherever he wanted. "Oh..."

"Ahem." Someone loudly cleared her throat. Someone standing right next to them.

Stevie opened her eyes. It was Anna, grinning from

ear to ear. Anna scraped another wooden chair on the floor, pulling herself up at their table with a great deal of commotion, as Stevie scrambled to get away from Owen and his wandering fingers. She almost tipped her chair over backward but she was out of his reach.

"Looks like you two are getting along great," Anna declared, slapping a folder down on the table near Owen's whirring tape recorder.

Lord, lord. If the nasty little seduction scene hadn't been bad enough in person, he had it on tape. He could rewind and listen whenever he wanted! *Are you going to kiss me or not, Mr. Dasher? Anyone who's read my book knows it's not that hard to get into my pants.*

Stevie grabbed for the thing, but Owen was faster. He had it turned off and stuck in his pocket before her hand hit the table.

"Just in case you needed any of the more recent figures on who's buying *Blissfully Single* or how well it's selling, I have that all for you," Anna announced, ignoring any of the subtext churning at the table. "We're very hot right now. In bookstores, I mean."

Hot. *In bookstores.* Uh-huh. Just like her. What had she been thinking, letting things get so out of hand? *Hand.* Bad choice of words. Why did everything remind her? His hand, her skirt. Her bad, bad judgment. Why couldn't she get her mind to move past their lewd and lascivious behavior?

Momentary lapse. Over. Move on, she ordered herself.

"Do you have any stats yet on how many marriages you've broken up?" Owen interjected in a perfectly charming tone that belied his words and annoyed her to no end.

"Broken marriages?" she echoed, stung by how

easily he could switch gears. "Me personally? Or the book?"

He arched one dark eyebrow. "The book, of course. I was wondering if anyone who was already married had decided to throw it over and join the *Blissfully Single* movement."

"Don't you think a marriage that can be broken up over a book deserves to fail?" Stevie returned, with more than a hint of acid. "Or do you think all marriages should stay glued together, no matter how terrible?"

"It doesn't matter what I think. It matters what you think. And what do you think, Stevie?"

He regarded her as if she were a rather dull exhibit at the zoo, mildly interesting, but nothing to write home about.

Okay, Mr. Smarty Pants. "You know what I think. You read the book."

"The book strikes me as superficial and not all that well thought-out."

"And once again, you don't have a question, just a sermon." Stevie stood up, ready to spit nails at him.

Superficial and not all that well thought-out. He had a lot of nerve coming to her signing, staring at her, witnessing her fans and their devotion, pawing her, teasing her with kisses that didn't happen and then, after all that, calling her book superficial. If she'd had a copy of *Blissfully Single* handy, she would've clobbered him with it.

"Is something wrong, Ms. Bliss?" he asked, feigning surprise, which only made her madder. He knew very well what reaction he was going to get. He was goading her into it. And she hated the idea that he could do that. She was supposed to be in control here, damn it.

"What exactly do you have against the ideas in *Blissfully Single?*" she demanded. "Are you that threatened by the notion that women can control their own lives?"

"You're getting off track."

"You pushed me there," she shot back.

"I don't think anyone pushes you anywhere," he said with what looked to her like a small sneer.

She came up with a sneer of her own. "That bothers you, does it?"

"Not in the least."

"Oh, yeah?"

"Yeah. Just for the record, I am not threatened by you, your book or the idea that women can control their own lives," he said evenly. "But I happen to be a big believer in truth, honesty, integrity. All those old-fashioned things that seem to have eluded you as you created this Stevie Bliss myth."

He was practically accusing her of being a fraud. And the best she could come up with was the most immature kind of "nyah, nyah" argument. Attempting to damp down her anger, losing the battle, she snapped, "I think we're done here, don't you, Mr. Dasher?"

"Stevie, can I speak to you, alone, for a second?" Anna broke in, plucking at her sleeve. "You wouldn't mind if we took a time-out, would you, Mr. Dasher?"

"Call me Owen," he said, once again doing a charm school routine for Anna. "No, I don't mind. Take your time."

Forcing a smile, Anna dragged Stevie over to the corner, about ten feet away. "Are you nuts?" she hissed. "You were yelling at the man. He is a reporter. We don't yell at reporters, okay?"

"He's a jerk. Accusing me of being a fake. And of breaking up marriages. Ha!" Turning herself firmly away from any position where she might have to see Owen Dasher, Stevie ground one spiked heel into the parquet floor. "First he's got his hand on my leg, like total sexual harassment..."

Anna lifted an eyebrow.

"Okay, so it wasn't sexual harassment," she admitted. She was a fair person. She could allow that much. "I let it happen. I encouraged it to happen. But I still think it's wrong that one minute he's all touchy-feely on my thigh and the next he's saying the book is shallow *and* a home-wrecker. That's pretty nervy, don't you think?"

"I think you can handle him." Anna pressed her lips together in a frown. "Stevie, you've had a thousand guys come on to you, and another thousand tell you your book was all wet, but you shot every one of them down without a problem. Why can't you do that this time?"

"He's different," she bit out. "He plays one way and then the other. He tried to seduce me just to distract me long enough to get a zinger in. The old bait and switch."

"Oh, my. A baiter and switcher. Call the cops," Anna responded, rolling her eyes.

"He's getting to me," she argued. "And not in a good way!"

"Calm down, okay? He's just trying to mess with your head." Anna continued in a soothing tone, "I told you, it doesn't matter. Whatever he writes, it's publicity, and it's for the good. You know the two big rules of media interaction—accessibility and quotability. Have you hit the target on either of those?"

She had certainly been accessible, given the fingers under her skirt, although she knew very well that was not the kind of accessibility Anna meant. And she was handing out quotes on the order of, "Oh, yeah?" Swallowing around a dry throat, Stevie allowed, "I am not hitting the target, no."

"So you're going to go back over there and give the sassy, quotable answers you want to give no matter what he asks, and then he'll write whatever he wants to write and we will go on from there. All right?"

"Yeah, yeah, I suppose."

Except Owen Dasher didn't wait for them to come back. He'd picked up his notes and his pen and whatever else he had hiding on his annoying body, and he came tromping over to interrupt their conversation.

"Sorry," he offered, acting all rushed and distracted. "My column's going to run on Wednesday this week, because of Thanksgiving, so I have an early deadline and I need to get out of here. Anyway, I think I have enough to put this one to bed...."

At which point Stevie began to choke and Anna had to pinch her arm hard to make her stop.

"Are you okay over there?" he asked solicitously.

"I'm fine."

"Right." He smiled. It was a humdinger of a smile, all toothy and wonderful and bright, and it made her want to strangle him. "Well, anyway, I'm okay with what I've got for Wednesday's column."

"Are you sure you don't need a few more quotes?" Anna asked anxiously. "We want to make your column as complete as it can be and for you to cover the whole range of ideas represented in Stevie's book. We don't want you to go away unsatisfied."

Stevie choked again.

"I'm satisfied," he said calmly, giving her and her obvious discomfort an amused glance. "But I'm thinking it might be fun to explore the *Blissfully Single* phenomenon in more depth. See it in action, so to speak."

"In action. Uh-huh," Stevie echoed, her mind filling with images of him and her and the kind of "action" the two of them could get into. Fighting. Kissing. Touching.

It was horrifying. Maybe strangling was too good for him.

"I'm thinking of the, uh, proposition you made before, Stevie."

"When was that?" she asked, not remembering anything remotely resembling a proposition except telling him it wasn't that hard to get into her pants. Was that a proposition? Or just temporary insanity?

"What are we talking about?" Anna interrupted briskly. "More interviews? Or maybe you'd like to observe the Blissfully Single lifestyle on its feet?"

"On its feet, off its feet, whatever." He smiled. She decided she hated him. "But nothing new planned for me. I wouldn't want to disrupt your schedule."

Right. He just wanted to disrupt *everything*, including her mental health.

He continued, "I think what would work best for me would be to follow Stevie around, on a typical day, maybe some time next week. If we're lucky, maybe we can stretch this into two or three columns. What do you say?"

"I think that is possibly the wor—"

"She'd love to," Anna cut in. "Fabulous idea."

"Anna!"

"It's great, Owen. Just give me a call and I'll set you up with her schedule for the next week or so. Anything you want, you have access."

And then the traitorous Anna stepped in front of Stevie, slipped him a business card, told him what hotel they were at, gave him her cell phone number and ushered him away, before Stevie could get in there and object.

More interviews with this guy? Following her around on a typical day? Breathing on her, touching her, pretending he was moving in for a kiss and then *not?*

"Not bloody likely," she said under her breath.

No way in hell she was getting anywhere near Owen Dasher ever again.

3

Bliss at the Bookstore
By Owen Dasher, *Chronicle* Columnist

When I went to see Stevie Bliss, the newest self-help maven, invade Chicago earlier this week, I expected Round Billion-and-one in the War of the Sexes. You know, men/bad, women/good, yadda, yadda, yadda.

Turns out Ms. Bliss is more into the *Game* of the Sexes. And when she puts up a pass, you can bet there will be a receiver. Lots of them. You see, that's a potent part of her offense. She looks for multiple receivers. To quote from her book, *Blissfully Single*, "Why limit yourself to one man? You're more likely to win if you play the field."

Good strategy, huh? Oh, and she knows how to kick the extra point, too. Right through the uprights.

Stevie Bliss 7, Chicago 0.

Who knew bookstores could be so much fun? Stevie Bliss, apparently. She's packed humor, moxie and a whole lot of steam into *Blissfully Single,* so it's no surprise she's a powerful package in person. As her assistant puts it, "Stevie bites." Ouch.

If I doubted that before I saw her in action, I

didn't after. Sure, she had some guys from the Swingin' He-Men Club stop by to give her a hard time. And the Righteous Moms Brigade, too.

But Ms. Bliss gave 'em all the old heave-ho, knocking out the competition with a few well-timed put-downs and an impressive display of pseudo S&M costuming. All this Leather Lady needs is a whip to really knock the crowd senseless.

Stevie Bliss 14, Chicago 0.

She says she's not anti-men or anti-marriage.

If that's what she wants me to believe, I'm not going to fight her on it. She might sizzle me with her dazzling blue eyes. She might walk on me with her spike heels. She might bring out the whip and make me beg for mercy. I'm only a guy, after all. I don't stand a chance....

"HEY, DASHER, nice column."

Startled, he glanced up from his computer screen. He'd thought he was alone in the newsroom. "I just sent it, T.J. You read it already? What are you doing here, anyway?"

T.J. was an intern who floated from department to department to fill a hole here or there. The staff reporters had figured out that she was very good at research and background material, and they kept her pretty busy doing grunt work they didn't want to. "I'm bored. I'm gonna be here late," she explained, ruffling her cropped orange hair with one hand. "I'm doing a round-up tonight for Sports. Lots of turkey tourneys."

"So you were just sitting there waiting for me to press Send, huh?"

"We're the only ones here. And I always like your stuff." She shrugged. "But I gotta tell you, I was expecting something different."

"Oh, yeah. Why?"

"When Mike or somebody said you were off to see Stevie Bliss at a bookstore, I thought, whoa, this is going to be good. But you weren't as snarky as I thought you'd be." She grinned. "You liked her, didn't you?"

"Uh, no."

"You did so," she teased. "Poor Dasher. Begging for mercy. Who ever thought we'd see Dasher goin' for the nasty girl? But he is totally smitten."

"I'm not smitten. I was making fun of her and the crowd's reaction to her." Owen concentrated on his computer screen. Surely there was something he needed to edit. "And she wasn't that nasty."

"Sure she was. I mean, she is." T.J. scooted around behind his desk, as if she planned to read over his shoulder. "It's not like it's a bad thing. Nasty girls are totally cool. Like Buffy, you know. Or Charlie's Angels."

"Isn't there something else you should be doing?"

"Nope. Just waiting for the Sports phone to ring."

"Okay. Well, you can wait back in Sports."

But she stayed where she was, continuing to scrutinize him.

Finally, he asked, "Is there something else?"

"Just curious. 'Cause I've read the book. *Blissfully Single*, I mean." She scooted closer. "After reading the book and then waiting to see what you said about her, I thought for sure you'd toast her."

Yeah, well, that was what he'd thought, too.

"You always flame the pop-culture dudes, y'know? So, good for you, for letting one slide."

He still wasn't sure he'd done the right thing. But there was something about Stevie Bliss... Something that had more to do with her brain than her ridiculously short skirt or her plunging neckline. Or even that wicked little moan she'd made when his thumb brushed the soft skin of her thigh. If he were a betting man, he'd lay odds she didn't even know she'd made that noise.

And that was what made it interesting. Everything else about her was so conscious, so planned. Except that noise. Now *that* was spontaneous.

He wasn't sorry he'd danced on the edge of impropriety to get her to make that tiny whimper, either. He'd been replaying it on his tape for hours.

Yet there was definitely more to his interest in her than an impromptu moan. It was the potent combination of brains and body, and the curious mix of audacity and innocence. Innocence? He must be mistaken. There was nothing innocent about Stevie Bliss, the leather-clad siren who strode into a room like she owned it, who slept with anyone who took her fancy, who had professional athletes for breakfast and politicians for lunch.

But the expression in her eyes when he touched her, and that amazing little noise...

She was a mystery, that was for sure.

"So, Dasher?" T.J. asked, interrupting his thoughts. "Why did you give her a bye? If you're not hot for her bod, I mean?"

Not hot for her bod? He was plenty hot. Maybe not *admitting* he was hot for her bod was more accurate. Or not sharing that fact with T.J., at any rate.

"Some of what she said made sense," he grumbled. "And I liked how she handled herself on her feet." He pushed back in his chair, eying the intern. "So you read the book? Did you buy into what she was saying, about playing the field and not getting tied down?"

"Sure. Well, not totally. I'm in no hurry to get married, that's for sure." T.J. plunked herself down in a nearby chair and gave herself a spin. "I think the one-month rule—you know, where your boyfriend automatically expires after a month, kind of like old milk?—that strikes me as cold. But it's a sharp idea if a few high schoolers look at their prom dates and go, hey, maybe I should go to college instead of getting married to this dweeb. Or even more so, chicks hitting twenty-five and getting all weird about not having a ring. Like the ones on... What was that terrible show, with all the women trying to get that one lame dude to marry them?"

"So you don't think it's demeaning for women to sleep around without being in love?"

"Demeaning? Who are you trying to kid?" She shrugged. "Men do it all the time. C'mon. Sex should be for fun. That's all she's trying to say. It's only when you try to pretend that love is involved that things get screwed up. So don't pretend. Let it be what it is and nobody gets hurt. Right?"

"That's the theory, anyway."

A phone rang from over in Sports, and she took off to answer. Backpedaling, she called out, "You need anything, you let me know, okay, Dasher? I'd love to work for you."

"Sure, sure." As he watched her pick up her phone across the wide newsroom, typing quickly onto her computer, he mused on her reaction. It seemed reasonable, after all, when she framed it like that. *Sex is for fun. It's only when you try to pretend that love is involved that things get screwed up.*

But could people—male or female—live that way? Could they really go around, taking whoever caught their fancy, without wanting something more?

It was a puzzle. And so was Stevie Bliss.

His mind replayed their encounter, including the little moan, without even bothering to listen to the tape. Amazing. And it wasn't just the question of how someone that bold could seem surprised or caught unawares by her own physical response. No, it was more about how she'd gotten to be Stevie Bliss.

Who was she, under all the prepackaged wrappings? Where had this *Blissfully Single* idea come from? Beautiful women didn't just wake up one day and decide they were never going to fall in love, never going to get married, without some kind of provocation. What happened to Stevie Bliss?

He certainly didn't have any answers from their short interview. It rankled that he was really a very good reporter and interviewer, and yet this time, he had done such a lousy job. What, had he asked a total of three questions? And all three were annoyance questions more than anything useful. *Never married, never left at the altar.* If she was telling the truth, that was the sum total of what he'd found out that he didn't already know from reading the book. Not a terribly complete personal profile.

If he got her in his crosshairs again, he would not let her off so easily.

When the intern pushed away from her terminal across the room, he said, "T.J., if you're still interested, I might have a project for you."

"Great. What do you need?"

"Some research."

Her lips curved into a smug smile. "Let me guess. Stevie Bliss."

He narrowed his eyes. "Yeah. You can start wherever you want. But I want to know her real name, which I am fairly certain is not Stevie Bliss. I want to know where she comes from, who she's dated, sisters, brothers, mom, dad, all that good stuff. Oh, and what she's got against underwear."

"I got it. The whole nine yards." T.J. gave him a knowing grin. "But you wouldn't by any chance be smitten or anything, right?"

"No," he returned tightly. "Just get me the info, will you?"

"Sure thing. It shouldn't even be that hard."

"I want everything you can find. Her kindergarten report card if you can find it."

"Yeah, yeah. I heard you the first time. First thing in the morning, I'm on it."

"Good." Maybe with a whole dossier in front of him, he could finally get a handle on Stevie Bliss.

Maybe.

"THERE IS NO WAY I am letting him follow me around for a whole day. I don't care how many times he calls or what you tell him. Not going to happen."

"You're driving me nuts about this," Anna muttered. She rose from the breakfast table in their suite, taking the newspaper with her, and then dropped into an overstuffed chair in front of the fireplace. After propping her feet up on the ottoman, she opened the newspaper and hid behind it.

Stevie announced, "If you want to convince me to do this, you're going to have to look at me."

Anna said nothing, just rumpled the newspaper loudly to indicate she wasn't listening.

Stevie glared at her friend. It was a wasted glare, since Anna was safely still behind the wall of newsprint. Feeling about as grumpy as she got, Stevie spun her spoon around her cup, aimlessly stirring black coffee.

Finally, after a long moment, Anna snapped down the paper. "I shouldn't have to convince you," she said tartly. "You should have enough of a brain to know this is a good idea. I mean, the biggest shopping season of the entire year is in full swing. You looked great on TV, we got a big bump from the first column, everyone else has run a line or two and now we're having trouble getting more coverage. He wants to do another column." She stopped, let out a small shriek of frustration, and then started again. "Christmas season, and she won't talk to a reporter. Yeah, sure, that makes perfect sense."

"It was a snide and distasteful column," Stevie announced grandly. She stood up, whipped her pink chenille robe around her matching flannel pj's, marched her fluffy pink slippers over to the chair opposite Anna and carefully took a seat.

"It was a perfectly wonderful column. And you know, you look ridiculous sashaying around like the Queen of Sheba in flannel pajamas with poodles all over them," Anna told her.

Stevie raised a finger. "Don't make fun of my pajamas. I've told you before. This is what I like to sleep in. And if I don't get my sleep, I won't have the energy to keep up the slutpuppy act."

"Flannel pj's and little braids in her hair and fluffy slippers," Anna mocked. "Oh, yeah, what a slut-puppy. I've been dressed for an hour and you're still lounging around in your poodle pajamas. I swear, Stevie, if anyone sees you in that Swiss Miss outfit..."

"Who's going to see me?" she demanded. "Oh, wait. The room service guy is probably calling in the scoop even as we speak."

Laying her head back into the cushions, Anna stared at the ceiling. "Why do I put up with this? I've turned into your nanny."

Momentarily considering whether she could throw something at Anna, Stevie wondered instead if there was time to call room service again and get them to bring up a big basket of chocolate croissants and another pot of coffee before she jumped into the shower and started on yet another day in what she was beginning to think of as "The Book Tour That Would Not End."

Outside the hotel, kids were drawing up their Christmas lists, grandmas were stoking up the oven to get a head start on holiday baking, parents were surfing toy stores for the season's hot buys and families were scouring lots looking for the perfect tree. But on the twenty-fifth floor of the Hotel Marceau, you'd never have known it was Christmas. No tree, no packages, not even a sprig of mistletoe.

She liked the suite, really she did. It was lush and comfortable, with a vaguely French château decor. But it was still a hotel. Being in a hotel at Christmas felt all wrong.

Moody and out of sorts, Stevie gazed into the flames crackling in the fireplace. She and Anna were doing what they did every day. Checking surveys, reading reports from focus groups, analyzing data and trying to stay one step ahead of all the other self-help gurus selling books this Christmas season. Bah humbug.

She was bored. She was hungry! And she could really have used that basket of chocolate croissants. Maybe she *did* have time to call room service....

The fantasy vanished quickly. Even if there were time, she couldn't go near pastries. Not if she wanted to fit into the size two Stevie Bliss wardrobe. She had worked so hard for so long, and the payoff of work-outs and body toning had been amazing. But she was starting to wonder if she was ever going to eat a hot-fudge sundae or sleep till noon or do anything fun ever again. What good was it to be a celebrity and make pots of money if you couldn't control your own schedule or what reporter you talked to or even your intake of croissants?

Maybe she was cranky all the time because she was seriously low on chocolate. Had anyone thought of that?

"Anna," she said firmly, "you're not my nanny. But you're not my boss, either. If I don't feel comfortable with that reporter, I shouldn't have to talk to him."

"Stevie—"

"I'm serious. He creeps me out."

"He does not." Anna sat up and threw down the newspaper. "That's the problem. You're attracted to him and it scares you. Well, get over it."

Her mouth fell open. "Attracted to him? You've got to be kidding!"

"You've got a thing for him, Stevie. Anybody in that bookstore could've seen it." She picked up the paper again and waved it. "And anybody who read his column knows he's also got a thing for you. He said you sizzled him with your dazzling blue eyes. He said he didn't stand a chance. Hmm, I wonder what that means? I'll tell you what it means. It means he has a thing for you. So use it to your advantage!"

"No." Stevie stayed where she was, resolute. "So what if he's whacked out by my faboo blue eyes? They're not even really blue."

Anna waved that off, too. "They'll be blue again as soon as you put in your contacts."

Stevie shook her head. "You're just not getting it. He's rude. He talked about me as if I were a football game. Paul Newman did that in that terrible movie, the one where he's in Paris and Joanne Woodward pretends to be..." She caught the look on Anna's face and cut it short. "Never mind. But I don't even like football!"

"So tell him to pick a different sport next time."

"And he said I wore dominatrix clothes. And that I carried a whip," she said angrily.

"He didn't say you carried a whip. He said you needed a whip. He was being satirical, Stevie. That's what he does."

"Not at my expense, he doesn't." Even though she knew it was dopey, she was still smarting over the "pseudo S&M" crack. Why did it matter if he thought she was all about kinky sex? Wasn't that why they dressed her that way?

No, she thought. *I'm supposed to project sex, but not ugly sex. And with a brain! Marlene Dietrich, not* Vampire Hookers from Outer Space.

Anna tried again. "Stevie, it's publicity. There are probably six or seven whip makers angling to sponsor you even as we speak. And if there are—"

But Anna didn't get to finish that thought. The phone rang, and they both jumped. For a moment they stared at it, merrily chirping away, all by itself on a delicate, gilt-edged table near the window. Since Anna handled everything on her cell phone, this was the first time Stevie could recall hearing that phony-looking French hotel phone ring. But ringing it was.

"It's eight o'clock in the morning," Stevie whispered. "Who'd be calling us now?"

"I'll get it." Stalking past the sofa, Anna grabbed the ornate black-and-gold phone out of its antique cradle and stuck it up to her ear. "Hello?" After a second or two, she began to relax, sinking into her Anna-the-Perfect-Assistant role. "Hello," she said smoothly. "Nice to hear from you. Thank you so much. Hang on a second, will you?" Covering the mouthpiece, she held out the receiver. "It's for you."

"Who is it?"

"Take a wild guess."

Stevie's stomach did a few flip flops. It couldn't be. "Dasher?"

"Well, it isn't Donner or Blitzen." Anna waggled the phone. "Come and get it."

"No."

"Stevie, don't be any more of an idiot than you already are. You're really very good at handling the press. So start handling, will you?"

She took the phone. "H-hello?"

"Good morning, Ms. Bliss. How are you today?"

That voice again. That damn voice that ruffled her nerve endings and weakened her knees. She squeezed her eyes closed and thought about the cold winter morning outside the frosted window. Chilly, chilly thoughts. It didn't help. She was already all melty.

"Stevie? Are you there?"

"It's awfully early, don't you think?" she asked, stalling for all she was worth. Maybe when it wasn't morning, she would have more wits about her. "Maybe you should call me back later. Like, this afternoon?"

"According to the schedule Anna sent me, you'll be speaking at the Brody Academy by then."

You gave him my schedule? she mouthed at her traitor of a best friend. Anna shrugged.

"Well, we're not really up and around yet, so this isn't a good time to talk. Anna and I were just having breakfast and—"

"Excellent." How did he make a regular old word like "excellent" come out so sensuous and sly? She leaned away from the receiver, blunting the impact of his voice a little, but she still caught it when he added, "I'm in the lobby, and I have a box of Krispy Kremes. So I'll come right up."

Although under normal circumstances she would've traded her soul for a doughnut, at the moment she was so shocked she passed right over the Krispy Kremes.

"You're in the lobby?" she demanded. "The lobby of my hotel? You just came over here and expected to come up to see me at eight o'clock in the morning?"

"I wanted to catch you before you left."

"You can't come up," she tried. "I'm not even dressed."

"Excellent," he said again, sounding so evil and self-possessed she wanted to throw the phone out the window. "I'd like to see the real, unvarnished Stevie Bliss."

"There is no such thing as an unvarnished Stevie Bliss," she shot back.

Anna snatched the receiver out of her hand. "Come right up. We're in the penthouse suite. The code for the elevator is 5-1." And then she dropped it back into the cradle.

"Anna!" Stevie cried. "Look at me! I'm wearing poodle pajamas! You invited him up here when I look like *this*?"

"He's the press. We need the press," her friend said flatly. "Accessible, remember?"

"That doesn't include my hotel room at eight o'clock in the morning."

"Come on, Stevie," Anna tried. "Just remember who you are. You're Stevie Bliss. You don't cower and hide when a lousy reporter throws you a curve. I don't see what you're getting so upset about. I have every confidence you will deal with him in the same confident and polished way you deal with everything else."

"I think you're starting to believe your own press releases, Anna," she groused. "What are you, sniffing toner when I'm not looking?" She pulled off her robe and kicked her slippers toward her bedroom, already unbraiding her hair. "Meanwhile, he's on his way up here and you said it yourself—I look like the Swiss Miss!"

"You've got a few minutes," Anna noted. "That elevator is slower than slow. And you don't have to get completely dressed. We can give him the sexy, at-home side of Stevie Bliss, lounging around in a seductive state of undress."

This was turning into a farce. She glanced down at

her cozy pajama top, buttoned up to her chin. "Since when does Stevie Bliss have a sexy, at-home side?"

"Since now." Anna took her hand and towed her into her bedroom. She frowned at the dresser. "I don't suppose you have anything slinky hiding under all the flannel in your drawers?"

Right behind her, Stevie moved to the closet, shoving one hanger after another across the rack. Tight tops. Tight skirts. Racy bits of designer outfits that didn't go together and didn't fit eight o'clock in the morning. And the minutes were ticking away. "The best I can offer is the hotel robe. But somehow I don't think big, fat white terrycloth with a Hotel Marceau insignia is going to do the trick."

"What about that silk robe the Barely Boutique gave you for signing at their store? What did you do with it?"

"Good idea." She scanned her memory for clues, hoping she'd stuffed it in her luggage somewhere when they left New York. "I think it's under..." Yanking open a suitcase at the back of her closet, she found two pairs of shoes and a white Barely Boutique bag containing the shocking pink robe she'd never worn. She held it up. The shape was basic, but the fabric and color were not. And it still had the price tags attached. Biting them off, she declared, "It'll have to do."

"Okay, good." Anna retreated, her hand on the door. "I'll keep him occupied till you get there. You try to do something with your hair and makeup. Oh, and don't forget the contacts."

Contacts. He was mad for her blue eyes, so she had to supply them. "Anna, this is out of control."

"Don't sweat it," her friend called out from the other room.

"How can I not sweat it?" she shouted back, peering intently into the mirror as she slapped in her contacts and reached for the eyeliner pencil. Getting it on without smudges or sticking herself in the eye would be a miracle.

Hovering in the doorway, Anna declared, "Stevie, I really think you need to calm down. I know you like to hide behind the outfits and the makeup, but you don't need them anymore. You have the act down without them. Maybe this will be exactly what you needed, to go with the flow, on the spur of the moment, to *be* Stevie Bliss instead of just *playing* Stevie Bliss."

"But, but—"

"Face it. You're ready. Three years ago, you would've fainted before you made out with someone like Owen Dasher in a bookstore."

"I didn't make out with him." *And I almost fainted.*

"It's kind of cool when you think about it. You're starting to live the life we've been promoting. So far, it's all been smoke," Anna said with more enthusiasm than Stevie really appreciated. "So maybe it's time for a few flames."

"What are you saying? He walks in, I jump him and have at him?" Abandoning the mirror, Stevie stripped off her pj's and slipped into the robe. *Brrr...*

"Of course not. The 'having at' part, I mean. Well, not unless you really want to. In which case, go for it. But please warn me so I can leave the room first."

"Anna!"

"All right, I'm kidding." Anna crossed her arms over her chest. "But you don't need to be afraid of him, either. If he flirts, flirt back. If he pounces, pounce back. It will be good for your reputation. And he's enough of a local celeb it would get great coverage."

"I don't think I'll be pouncing any time soon."

"Okay, well, I can live with that. I mean, there is a downside. If you pounced, had sex and then dumped him, which you would have to, to maintain any credibility as a blissful single, he might harbor bad feelings. And he does have a forum for his side of things." Anna shrugged. "Might be sticky."

"Don't even think about it. No pouncing, no sex, no nasty breakup." She frowned down at the robe. It really was not a good fit, with sleeves that were too long and a deep vee in the front where the slippery folds of fabric kept separating no matter how many times she tried to overlap it. Besides, even wrapped in all that fabric, she felt naked and bizarre.

She had lost a lot of her modesty over the past few years, dressing like Stevie, but still...

"Are you sure about this?" she asked doubtfully, cinching up the sash. "I mean, it's not the dominatrix look, that's for sure, but it's not the seductress at home, either. More like slutty housewife looking to score with the refrigerator repairman. *The Postman Always Rings Twice*, y'know? The gross Jessica Lange version, not Lana Turner."

"I don't know what that means, and I don't care. You look fine. You told him you weren't dressed. What does he expect?" As they both heard the knock on the door, her friend turned. "Okay, there he is. Don't forget your glasses. Don't forget to be accessible and quotable. And shake your hair."

"Yeah, yeah." Good thing the Stevie Bliss trademark hair was fairly disheveled to start with. She frowned at herself in the full-length mirror. There were so many things wrong with this picture. No armor. No weapons. Just the girl herself, bare and shivering under a too-big, too-pink robe.

But there was no time to worry. *He* was here. She could hear him chuckling with Anna out in the main living room of the posh suite. Feeling like a prisoner on her way to the guillotine, she ran her hands through her hair, roughing it up into more of a mane, and tried to think like a lion. Aware he could see her bedroom door from the living room, she took a step into the short hallway and shut the door firmly behind her, putting a wall in between him and the pink poodle pajamas of her real life.

I am a lion and he is... Not.

It was the best she could do. And then she threw back her shoulders, took a deep breath and prepared to greet Owen Dasher. *No pouncing, no sex, no nasty breakup*, she reminded herself. Yeah, she could do that.

4

THE MOMENT SHE SAW HIM, lounging there in the living room with Anna, Stevie began to rethink her good intentions. No pouncing? No sex? No *nothing*?

The man really was way too gorgeous for his own good. Or for *her* good, anyway. Especially for this early in the morning. He was wearing a soft black sweater with a line of white collar visible at the neck, charcoal pleated pants and a black wool jacket, with a longer camel-colored overcoat draped over his arm. Pulled-together, classy and warm. All the things she wasn't.

It was unfair. Especially when he had a box of Krispy Kremes with him, and she could smell them from here. The perfect man, and he smelled like sugar and butter and baked goods. Pangs of hunger rose inside her. One, big, delicious, melt-in-your-mouth man....

He turned. He saw her. And she edged closer, drawn by the tantalizing prospect of a man and his doughnuts.

But Anna swept in and took away the box and his coat, mumbling something about hanging it up and finding a plate for the Krispy Kremes. Stevie barely noticed. Owen and his mesmerizing green eyes were in the way.

"Good morning," he offered, his gaze tracing a

path from her head to her toes, lingering on the place where her robe gapped in the front, exposing a fair expanse of bare skin. Stevie quickly crossed her arms over her chest, which made things worse, pushing everything together and giving her an unfortunate amount of cleavage. His eyes widened.

Awkwardly, she covered herself as best she could, leaving one arm wrapped loosely across while sort of tapping her opposite shoulder with the other one, trying to seem all nonchalant and natural. *Very smooth, Stevie*, she told herself. *Talk about a geek!*

"You weren't kidding, were you? You did just tumble out of bed." He paused, still studying her. "Or maybe you concocted this rumpled look for my benefit?"

Tumbling out of bed...Owen Dasher half-naked amidst tangled sheets, extending a hand to reel her back in... Her brain fed her a cavalcade of wicked images, and she could feel heat suffuse her cheeks. If she didn't nip this in the bud, everything from her forehead to her navel would glow the same hot pink as her robe.

"No, I didn't just tumble out of bed." She curved her lips into a determined smile, smashing her hands into her pockets, holding the robe together firmly. "And believe me, at this hour, I'm not concocting anything for you or anyone else." *Liar, liar, pants on fire. From Swiss Miss to* The Postman Always Rings Twice *in thirty seconds.* "I like to be comfortable, that's all, while I lounge around, read the paper, have my coffee. You know, all those normal everyday things."

"I see." But his eyes were glued to a point somewhere between her neck and shoulder. What was that all about?

"Is there a reason you're staring?"

"No. It's just that..." He moved in closer, winding a few tendrils around his fingers. She held her breath. *He's touching my hair.* Such a small gesture, with a thin strand of golden hair twined between his fingers. But incredibly intimate.

She was very aware of each breath, as her breasts rose and fell against the cool silk, her nipples peaking in the chilly hotel room. No need to ice anything down today. Her nipples were up and ready to greet visitors.

How odd to feel so naked when she had so much fabric wrapped around her. But the silk robe may as well have been made of tissue paper. It was no protection at all.

Stevie swallowed. Owen's face tipped in, so breathtakingly close to her own that she closed her eyes and held herself very still, ready to sink into the sensation if he wanted to kiss her or—even more intoxicating— slip his hands inside her robe.

But instead he murmured, "It's very strange. Your hair seems to be bent."

Bent? Batting his hand away, she reached for the spot he'd touched, feeling the place where a piece of hair stuck out at a funny angle. She spun on her heel, frowning, wondering where the nearest mirror was. *Oh, hell.* She looked awful. Here she'd been mooning over the intimacy of his fingers tangled in her hair, and he was probably contemplating how closely she resembled the Scarecrow. *If I only had a brain.*

The worst part was how easy it was for him to keep her off balance. Just when she thought she was operating with confidence and pizzazz, Ms. Sexy Thang, he pointed out that she had *Hee Haw* hair. And she was back to square one. When she looked in the mirror, she saw self-conscious, clumsy Stephanie Blanton.

She hated feeling like that. She was past that stage, damn it. Stephanie, no more.

Running her fingers through her hair to try to smooth it, she sent a gloomy look across the room at Anna, who was emerging from the kitchen with the plate of doughnuts. Stevie grimaced, trying to telegraph how poorly this was going, how quickly her self-esteem had sunk.

Motioning that she should quit fooling with her hair, Anna gave her a thumbs-up, mouthing "accessible" and "quotable," which didn't help in the least. Stevie shook her head as an answer. But Anna walked on by, clearly intent on transporting the platter of Krispy Kremes to the breakfast nook.

"Hmm," Owen mused, peering at her. He made a half turn, glanced at the bedroom door down the hall, the one she'd closed behind her, and then wheeled back to look at her again. "I think I'm getting the picture."

"What picture?"

"Hair a mess, makeup smudged, as if it's left over from last night, no glasses..."

No glasses? *Ooops.* As for the smudged makeup, that was just early morning ineptitude. "Well, I..." she began, trying to think of some explanation.

"It seems obvious. You had a long night, didn't you?" Looking very suspicious, he backed away from her. "And I noticed you were careful to close the bedroom door. So is that it? You shared a long, hot night with Mr. December and he's still in there, hiding under the covers while you come out and talk to me?"

She almost laughed out loud at that one. He thought she had a stud hiding in her bedroom, when all she had was flannel poodle pajamas.

Now it was her turn to be coy. After all, she was a smart girl. She saw the curl in his lip and the sneer he was giving that closed door. Was he jealous? Could she possibly be that lucky?

"So, who's Mr. December?" he asked darkly. "What mental midget have you latched on to this time? Is he over twenty-one?"

Woo-hoo! She *could* be that lucky. He thought she'd slept with some stupid boy toy right under his nose and it ticked him off. *Advantage, Stevie.*

"Mental midget, huh?" Chin up, a sparkle in her eye, she inquired, "Do you really think Bill Gates would turn me down?"

"Just tell me who it is."

"Well, I can't do that." She shrugged. "Because that information wouldn't be any of your business, would it? The identity or even the age of Mr. December, I mean."

"I need to tell my readers if your month is already booked or if you're still taking offers," he tried.

"Still taking offers," she said sweetly.

"Good to know."

"Good." Now that she knew he was jealous, she felt back in control. Her inner Stevie came roaring to the forefront. She shook her hair, carefree and wild, looking forward to bantering the morning away, if that's what he had in mind.

"Why don't you two sit down?" Anna, now doughnut-free, maneuvered the two of them away from the hall and back into the main living room part of the suite. "I'm sure Owen has things he wants to ask and you have things you want to say, *messages* you want to convey," she stressed. "Conversation will be easier if you sit down and have some coffee. Relax."

But they both stood there, eyeing each other. There was no way Stevie planned to sit down if he didn't. She didn't fancy looking up at Owen Dasher.

"I'm not hungry. Or thirsty," she said evenly. "And I like standing."

In a more dire tone, Anna added, "Maybe the caffeine or the sugar will help you get your brain working. Which would be a very good thing right about now. Because you aren't really staying on topic, are you?"

"I think we drank all the coffee earlier. There isn't any."

"So you two have a seat and I'll call down and order some more." With one last warning glance, practically begging Stevie to play nice, Anna rushed off to the phone by the window.

Determined to stay ahead in the game this time, Stevie led Owen to the breakfast table, which was set into a small area on the far side of the living room. At the last moment, however, she changed her mind, decided it would be safer if they were separated by the larger table in the suite's dining room, did an abrupt about-face, and crashed right into the hard wall of his chest.

An "oof" sound escaped her as she found herself plastered up against him. His hands braced her shoulders, steadying her, but also drawing the sides of the robe farther apart, revealing even more skin than before. He moved a finger to trace the line of silk along her collar, sliding down, now so very close to her breast, making her tremble with *wanting*. As her body flushed with warm color, she felt hot and cold at the same time, anything but steady. He was so close. She was so hungry for more of his touch, more of his...everything.

"What are you waiting for?" she whispered, brushing her palm over the hard angle of his shoulder, tilting her head, closing her eyes, holding herself ready for his lips and his hands.

This time, surely he would kiss her. Surely...

"You are something else," he murmured, and she couldn't remember how to breathe for just a second. *It was going to happen. It had to happen.*

A small, eager sound escaped her, somewhere in the neighborhood of a whimper. And his hands immediately dropped away from her robe. She opened her eyes, in time to see Owen, holding himself rigid, step back, leaving a three-foot safety zone between them. It was as if she carried some dread disease communicable by air. Just because she made a little noise?

Bereft. Alone. Unkissed. *Unfair.*

She swallowed. Men weren't supposed to turn down her advances. They weren't supposed to make her feel like an idiot. Wasn't that the whole idea of Stevie Bliss, to be in the driver's seat and not dependent on what *they* wanted? Great theory. Didn't seem to work, however.

Damn him, anyway, for upsetting her applecart one more time.

"So sorry," she murmured, pulling herself together, adjusting her robe to a more respectable position.

"Not at all." He gave her a wide berth as she edged around him, leading the way to the wide, polished cherry table in the dining room.

"Have a seat."

"Ladies first."

Hmm...So he wanted to make this as chilly and formal as a diplomatic summit at the Kremlin. Fine. She sat.

As cheerfully as she could manage, she declared, "Well, Mr. Dasher, this is your tea party. Fire when ready."

"Yes, Ms. Bliss." Taking the seat directly across from her, he checked his notes, not meeting her eyes. "Since we already brought up the subject of Mr. December, maybe you can tell me how you came up with that scheme. One man per month, I mean."

"Certainly. It's not based on anything scientific, just personal observation."

Actually, it was market-driven, like everything else about *Blissfully Single*. When asked how long they thought they could date a woman without one or the other becoming bored with the relationship, a majority of men aged 18 to 25 who were surveyed answered a month or less. And in this case, what was good for the gander was good for the goose. Stevie had no intention of sharing that information, however.

"It fits my personal experience," she said coolly. "After a month, I find I've had enough. We start to bicker, he starts to get clingy and talk about moving in... It's so dreary. But the funny thing is, if the man knows he only gets a month, I mean, if we set that out right at the beginning..." Leaning forward across the table, she offered her naughtiest smile. "He tries harder."

"In what way?"

Accessible. Quotable. At this point, malicious and downright mean were more her style. She wanted to make her words hurt Owen Dasher. If he was bothered by the idea that she had a guy in her room right now, what would he do if she embroidered on the fantasy?

"In bed," she told him, enjoying the little twitch in his jaw when she said "bed." "It's like they know I've been with someone else immediately before them, and the next guy is just around the corner. So they want to make it memorable. They try harder. Lots *harder.*"

"I see," he said tersely.

"And the things they come up with..." She widened her smile, propping her chin in one hand, enjoying torturing him. "Men are so funny. Everything's a competition. Which is wonderful for me. It's led to some creative and entertaining sexual adventures. Simply *amazing.*"

She pretended to shiver, hoping she wasn't going over the top. But, no, Owen still looked as if he were buying it, hook, line and sinker. So she went on, improvising, improving on the basic idea. "Why, I remember the time I met a professional football player at a party and we hooked up that same night. It was only that one time, so I don't even recall his name. No, it wasn't just once. It was at least twice. Or maybe I'm getting him confused with someone else. But I think he was a tight end."

As Owen made a choking sound, she batted her baby blues, vamping it up big time, enjoying herself immensely. *Payback time, Mr. Dasher. Compare me to a football game, will you? Call me a fake, will you? Get me to the point where I'm putty in your hands and then back away, will you?*

All innocence, practically licking her lips, she asked, "Is there a football position called a tight end?"

"Yes," he managed between clenched teeth.

Poor dear. "He had these incredible thighs." She sculpted these imaginary thighs in the air. "Athletes, whew. The pecs, the abs...and the muscle control. Incredible. You wouldn't think a football player would be that clever. The stereotype may be all brawn and no brains, but this guy was brilliant when it came to bed games. The ideas he had—"

"I got it."

She lifted her shoulders, letting the slippery silk slide over her skin. "It was all in good fun. And it was. *Very* fun. What does *punt* mean, anyway? I mean, I know what he told me it meant, as far as where he wanted to—"

"I don't really need the details," he said acidly. "I write for a family newspaper, you know."

Stevie was really hitting her stride now. And if Owen's collar seemed to be a little too tight, if that nerve in his jaw kept jumping, well, he had no one to blame but himself. "So far, I have to say that the one-month system is working out great." She sighed with delight over her made-up memories. "We meet, we peak, we part. Quick, neat, easy for everyone. What's not to like?"

"And exactly how many men would that be?" he inquired, with just enough of an edge that she knew she still had him. "How many men have you met, peaked with and parted from, I mean?"

"Oh, I don't know," she said carelessly. "It's not like I'm keeping track. Hmm... How many men have even lasted the month? A month is my max, you know, not *de rigeur*. Most don't get that far. They have to be really, really good to get the whole month."

"Any repeat customers?"

"I'm not sure I understand you." *Customers* sounded like he thought she was a hooker.

"Anybody good enough to stick around more than one month?" he explained, looking very dark and disturbed.

"Not yet," she answered sweetly, deciding on the spur of the moment to abide strictly by the rules of her fictional Guy-a-Month Club. Besides, it was also strictly true. If there hadn't been any one-month lovers, then no one had stuck around for longer than that, either, had they?

"How old are you?" he asked, his pen poised over his notebook. He'd shifted gears so quickly, it caught her by surprise.

"Twenty-seven. Does it make a difference?"

He persevered. "Aren't you a little young to have given up on marriage and children?"

"I have plenty of time to repent my evil ways and change my mind, don't I?"

"Do you?"

"Yes. Besides," she pointed out, "I never said I was giving up on children. Adoption, insemination... Or a friendly neighborhood sperm donor. There are options outside marriage." She tipped her head to one side. "Should I put you on the list of possible sperm donors in case my biological clock starts ticking?"

But he ignored her. "Where were you born?"

She sat up, trying desperately to remember what she was supposed to say. She and Anna had fought over just the right place to stick in her bio, somewhere difficult to trace and yet exotic enough to be interesting. But what was it? What with Owen and the early hour and the whole Mr. December fantasy, her mind had gone blank. Great time to have a mental block on something as basic as a birthplace.

Where was Stephanie born? Omaha, Nebraska. Not the right image.

Where was Stevie born? In a bar outside Washington, D.C., when she and Anna had conceived the idea. But she could hardly say that. On the other hand, how could she explain not knowing her own birthplace?

"Samoa," she told him, pulling it out of thin air. She was freezing, so somewhere warm sounded nice. Was it warm in Samoa?

"Samoa?"

She shrugged. "My parents were in the Peace Corps." Totally untrue. But it explained Samoa.

"College?"

"Yes," she answered politely.

"Where?" She could tell he was losing his patience and she actually wasn't provoking him on purpose this time.

"Actually, I went to several. I had trouble deciding where I wanted to be and what I wanted to major in." Also a lie. She'd known since she was six she wanted to be in marketing.

"But you don't have any background in sociology or psychology or anything that might back up what you say in *Blissfully Single?*"

"Nothing whatsoever," she said cheerfully. "I'm just naturally in tune with today's woman, I guess."

"And what did your parents do?"

"They still do. They're both college professors, actually. Not in Samoa." Wow, she'd let a little bit of reality slip through. When she wasn't paying attention, she actually did tell the truth occasionally. "They've lived a lot of different places. Their field is kind of narrow and they're in demand."

"What field?"

"Excuse me?" She met his gaze, not sure where this was going. "Why do you want to know about my parents?"

"Are they married?"

"Yes, of course."

"Happily?"

"I suppose so." What was he getting at?

"So this *Blissfully Single* thing isn't a reaction to your parents' lousy marriage?"

Oh, please. "You find someone you don't understand, so you try to pigeonhole her into the most easily available slot, is that it?"

Once again, he paid no attention to her question. "I'm curious—what do your parents think of you and your hot and cold running sex partners?" He arched a dark eyebrow again, all cool disdain. "My mom certainly wouldn't appreciate me blabbing about the gory details of my love life."

She cooed, "And does your love life have gory details? Do tell."

"You're avoiding the question."

"What do they think of me and my hot and cold running sex partners? Hmm... If they knew, which they don't, neither of them would care in the least." She pushed her chair a few inches away from the edge of the table.

"Really?"

"Really." It was the last word she intended to offer on the subject of her parents, the smart, intellectual, drier than three-day-old toast Blantons, who'd never met an obscure indigenous culture they didn't love.

Their daughter... Well, if they remembered they had a daughter, she'd be surprised.

But being Owen Dasher, he had to push it, didn't he? "It wouldn't embarrass a couple of college professors to know their daughter was now the sex kitten of the Western World?"

"Trust me on this," she said very slowly and carefully, so he would be sure to catch every word. "They wouldn't recognize me in a line-up. And if it were brought to their attention that their daughter was the sex kitten of the Western World, which, by the way, I'm not, neither of them would turn a hair. They would look you straight in the eye and say, 'Fascinating.' And then they would start filling you in on the range of sexual practices common among extinct tribes on the subcontinent until you wanted to tear your hair out."

"So that's your story?" He pulled his chair closer to the table. "Emotionally distant parents raise lonely little girl who engages in purposely shocking behavior, still craving their attention and approval?"

She exhaled. There was nothing wrong with her parents, just that they were in their own world, which didn't seem to have much room for her. "I'm from Venus. My parents are from Pluto. They're perfectly lovely people. But they're also your classic absentminded professors."

"Okay, well, this is interesting. I'm getting a more complete picture of Stevie Bliss here."

She could tell. He thought he had her pegged as some cliché Freudian basket case who hated her parents and wanted to rebel by turning into a poor, downtrodden slut, a user and a loser. Which was all wrong.

Frowning, Stevie tried to steer them back onto the ground she wanted to cover. "Don't make too many assumptions." She laid both palms flat against the smooth wood of the table, regarding him sternly. "I happen to have been born with a very strong sense of who I am and what I want. I am more than happy to depend upon myself and not feel the need to create some slurpy, phony family unit for support. I believe each of us is unique and different, and we each should decide for ourselves what and who we need to be. It's not about who your parents are or what they did or didn't do when you were six. It's about you. About what you can become if you give yourself a chance."

There. Anna would be proud. Perfectly on message.

All Owen Dasher did was flip the top closed on his pad. "Yeah, I read that in the book somewhere." He checked his watch, getting more remote by the minute. "So, listen, I guess I'll take off now. If I need anything else, I'll be in touch." Rising, he inclined a thumb in the direction of her bedroom, offering cynically, "Wouldn't want to leave your hunk o' the month alone too long."

He was leaving. Just waltzing out as if none of the tension, none of the electricity between them, had ever existed. *Liar.* She leapt to her feet, leaning across the table. "Mr. December will keep."

"Will he?" He gazed at the door. "So why is he afraid to come out? Is he married? Underage? The Elephant Man?"

"None of the above. But his privacy is important to him." She knew men. She knew what would twist the knife of male envy. "You know rock stars. He has his fans to consider."

"A rock star, eh? And will he get a whole month?"

Owen inquired, his green eyes steady on her face. "How long will he last on the Stevie Bliss carousel? A week? Maybe an hour?"

Oooh, he was pushing his luck. "He was pretty good," she allowed. "I think I'll at least have him back for an encore. Or maybe I'll just wander back in and take my encore now."

Owen's face clouded with disgust. "I can't believe you—"

"How's it going?" Out of nowhere, Anna swooped in. She'd probably been eavesdropping, waiting till things got ugly. "Leaving so soon?"

"Yeah, I have to be somewhere."

"Did you get what you need for another column?" Anna chirped. "We're happy to set up another meeting if not."

"I'm not sure yet." His gaze flickered over Stevie, and he shook his head.

"You could always drop by the girls' school later," Anna said helpfully. "If you needed more material, I mean. We would love another column. And you did say you wanted to see Stevie in action."

"And what could I expect to hear at the Brody Academy?" he asked. "You planning to preach the same brand of sex with strangers to the kiddies?"

"I guess you'll just have to show up to find out, won't you?" Stevie stood, jerking her belt tighter. She spun on her bare heel and whipped around the far side of the table, heading back to snare a doughnut before she thought better of it. "Anna," she called out over her shoulder. "You'll see our pal the reporter out, won't you?"

"Sure," Anna put in nervously. "I'll just, uh, get your coat."

"Thanks," he returned in a clipped and angry tone.

Stevie grabbed a Krispy Kreme and took a huge bite. The hell with her perfectly toned abs and her skinny thighs. After the morning she'd had, she needed fat and sugar, pronto.

After some murmurs she couldn't quite get the gist of, she heard the door shut, and then Anna returned, chewing her lip. "Should I ask?"

"Don't even start with me. I'm on, I'm off, I'm on again, I'm cruising and then he looks at me like yesterday's mashed potatoes." She took another huge bite of doughnut. "I don't know what he's up to or what he wants or what the hell he's going to write about me in that damn column of his. I told him, basically, go for it, take me, I'm yours, and he backed off. He backed off!"

Anna sat down, hard. "No."

"Yes!" she cried. "He turned me down. Flat. So then I tried to get him totally hooked by making up stories about my hot lovers. I stole the idea from *Love in the Afternoon*. You know, with Audrey Hepburn."

"Not movies again," Anna said ominously.

"Never mind. It didn't work. Or maybe it did. Maybe that's the problem." Stevie dropped the doughnut back on the plate. "Being around him is like... Like playing Ping-Pong with a naked satyr."

"If I'm supposed to understand that, I don't."

"Yeah, well, I don't, either." She let out a huge, aggrieved noise, somewhere between a scream and a groan. "He drives me nuts! I want to sleep with him. I want to *lick* him. I want to punish him. All at the same time!"

"Sounds kind of kinky," Anna suggested, her eyes lighting up.

"Not nearly kinky enough." Stevie threw herself onto the sofa. "He disrespects me, he thinks my ideas are beneath contempt, and I still want him. What is wrong with me?"

"I don't know. But be careful, okay?" Anna patted her on the top of the head. "You're good at this, but you're not Wonder Woman. I may have underestimated him. Maybe staying away is the best idea after all."

"I think it's too late," she groaned.

"But that's good, right? It's too late because he's really into you?"

No, because I'm into him. Her robe had twisted under her when she tossed herself onto the sofa, and she debated ripping the damn thing off and throwing it into the fireplace. What a disaster this morning had been. And she blamed the robe.

"Well?" Anna prompted. "Is he into you?"

"Not exactly. It's more like he's decided I'm a puzzle," she explained, remembering the funny looks he kept sending her. She knew he was jealous there for a while, and yet he seemed to be disgusted later. It was as if the very thing that intrigued him annoyed him, too. And who could figure that out? "He seems to have decided I need to be analyzed or examined or something."

"That's not good."

"Not good at all," she said gloomily, punching a pillow. "He wants me because I'm a slut. But he doesn't *want* to want me. Because I'm a slut!"

Anna's brows drew together. "I don't get it."

"Neither do I," Stevie murmured. "Neither do I."

OWEN HAD HIS CELL PHONE out before he cleared the lobby. "Is T.J. around?" he barked. "I need to talk to her."

As he stomped out of the Hotel Marceau, putting its Country French decor behind him, T.J. picked up. He didn't give her a chance to say anything after "hello."

"I have some info on Stevie Bliss," he said curtly. "She says her parents were in the Peace Corps but now they're college professors, both in the same field, something like anthropology. She claims to be twenty-seven, and she may or may not have been born in Samoa. I think she was lying about the Samoa part." He paused. "Or she may be lying about all of it."

"Okay," T.J. said breathlessly. "I'll see what I can do."

Moodily, he added, "I also need to know what rock stars are in town."

"Barry Manilow," she offered.

"Not Barry Manilow." He couldn't believe what he was reduced to. He almost considered camping out outside the Hotel Marceau just to see if anyone he recognized walked out. This woman was making him crazy. He'd never had this much trouble putting a profile together. But it seemed like the more he tried to figure her out, the slipperier she got. "Find out, okay? Make a list. Especially any rock musicians playing Chicago who were unaccounted for this morning."

"I'll try," she said doubtfully.

"Good. Call me if you find out anything." He made up his mind on the spur of the moment. "I have some errands to do this morning, and then I'll try to swing by the office. And then..." He clenched his jaw. "Then I have to go to the Brody Academy."

"Brody? The chichi girls' school? Doesn't sound like your kind of place."

"It is now. There's this mystery I have to get to the bottom of."

A mystery named Stevie Bliss.

5

GIVEN THEIR LAST contentious encounter, he hadn't expected to be so happy to see her again. But there she was, her usual feisty self in her too-short skirt and bad-girl boots, and his heart took a little leap. Before he could stop it, he found himself grinning like a baboon.

That had to go. He canned the smile, opting instead for a semi-scowl, determined to control himself better around Stevie.

The girl had moxie, he'd give her that. Before he got here, he'd wondered if she would dress more conservatively or behave with more decorum based on her audience. Nope. She went for it. Stevie Bliss taking her hotter-than-thou road show into a high school was pretty audacious. He didn't know whether to be outraged, that someone like that was setting herself up as a role model for teens, or impressed that she had the guts to try. And he wondered how the parents of these girls were going to react once they found out who exactly was counseling their children.

He contemplated a very dark idea. What if he wrote a column, acting all shocked and surprised that the notorious Stevie Bliss was offering pointers to innocent teenage girls on how to run their love lives? It might be kind of amusing. Hoisting Stevie with her own petard. He'd like to hoist her...

Lose that thought, he ordered himself.

Digging into scandals and exposing less than savory conduct was, after all, what he did for a living. He didn't think of himself as a muckracker, not even a social reformer. Just a guy who told the truth, who brought stories to the public that they needed to know about. Some of those stories were funny or strange, some sad, but they were all intended to help his readers—and himself—understand more about the world they were living in.

Did the public need to know about Stevie Bliss? Or was this more of a personal agenda?

His scowl deepened. He'd never been the kind of reporter who came in with an agenda, but maybe this would be a good time to break that rule. As long as he only used her real words as ammo, that was fair, wasn't it? Or maybe not. His ethics seemed to be flying out the window, and he didn't like what that said about him.

From his seat at the very back of the Brody Academy auditorium, tucked into a dark corner, Owen knew she couldn't see him. It felt right to be back in a familiar role of skeptical observer, sitting there with his notebook on his knee, instead of becoming part of the story, as he always seemed to do when he took on Stevie one-on-one. What was it about her that made him throw away every good reporter's instinct he had, and instead act more like an opponent than an observer? Whatever it was, he sure hoped he got over it pronto.

Right now, he wanted to fling enough words at her to get her to wake up and behave. Not likely. Not healthy, either. And yet, he had this overwhelming desire to puncture that bad-girl veneer.

Who are you? he wondered, staring at her.

As the only man in the room, he received a curious glance or two from the teachers and students sitting nearby, but he didn't mind. Actually, he was glad to be the only representative of his gender present. It meant that Stevie's lay-a-bed rock star lover, if there was one, had other fish to fry this afternoon. Or maybe this mythical person didn't want to be spotted acting like a Stevie Bliss groupie. Owen fumed, flipping his notes to the list T.J. had come up with. So far, he had a choice of Bob Dylan, David Bowie and some group called Planet Poo and the Poo Dogs. Too old, too married and way too weird. It was disgusting imagining Stevie making her little moans for any of them.

That idea made Owen's scowl deepen. Stevie with a rock star boyfriend. Pah. If that didn't sound made-up, he didn't know what did. So why did the idea eat away at him like this?

Even glowering and sending out bad vibes, he felt sure he was mostly unnoticed. The women and girls in the audience seemed far more curious about Stevie. He saw a glimpse or two of the roving Anna, lurking somewhere behind the scenes, but she hadn't caught sight of him, either. He had successfully faded into the shadows of the last seat in the back row, and it felt good.

Eschewing the podium and the microphone, Stevie stood in front of the stage and talked up-close-and-personal to the senior class from the Brody Academy. His heart seemed to twist when he saw her smile at the crowd. Pen poised, Owen waited to take down a few pithy quotes he could use against her later.

Maybe the bit about the whipped cream and cherries if she tried that one again.

"I'm not going to stand up here and rag on about me," she announced. "Because you're not me. And I'm not going to give you a whole list of rules and regulations to follow, either, like each and every one of you is the same and the same list would work for all of you. Who needs that?"

She waited, and the girls looked at each other and their teachers, not sure what they were supposed to do. "I'm serious," Stevie went on. "Who needs that? How many of you need one more person telling you what to do? Show of hands."

There were a few giggles, maybe even a gasp, but no one raised a hand. "I thought so," she told them. "You go to a great school, you're brighter and more savvy than I ever was and you look to me like smart cookies who know your own minds. And here's a little secret—all the fun is in choosing, in daring, in clearing a path and taking it. But remember, once you're in charge, you have both opportunity *and* responsibility. I think you will find out that the opportunities are so awesome, all the responsibility is worth it, too."

Well, nothing salacious so far. Instead, she sounded like a graduation speaker. Like another Chicago newspaper columnist, he half expected her to tell them to remember to wear sunscreen. Disappointing.

As she wound her way through the crowd, asking questions, making it more of a chat session than a speech, the girls grew more animated, asking questions and offering opinions, disagreeing with Stevie and with each other, each adding her views on marriage and children and careers, even sex, with a frankness that amazed him. Some were thoughtful, some were silly and some were downright ridiculous, but Stevie listened and commented on every one, stressing again and again that each different angle was valuable, that each girl's unique voice was important.

Having choices in life, encouraging diversity and free thinking, aspiring high and achieving higher, not being afraid of fear... Not exactly controversial. She even told them not to confuse sex with love, and not to do anything they didn't want to just because someone else tried to push. Huh.

"Your whole lives are ahead of you," she said breathlessly, her eyes sparkling as she *hugged*—actually reached out and hugged—a teen. "I know you've heard that a million times, but it's still true. The excitement is just beginning for you."

If she weren't careful, she'd start to get misty, he thought cynically. He noticed that she had lost her husky come-hither voice somewhere along the line, that she never once flashed cleavage or mentioned her underwear situation, she didn't tell them to drop their boyfriends after thirty days and she kept her mouth shut about her own sexual adventures.

Yeah, she saved that info to torture poor, unsuspecting reporters.

"Dasher, you are losing it," he muttered. Some hard-boiled newsman. Instead, he was once again worrying about the number of notches in Stevie Bliss's bedpost.

He narrowed his eyes, trying to decide once and for all whether she was sincere or this was all staged. Because he still had a hard time accepting that someone who sounded as flippant and unfeeling as she did in her book, someone who bragged about bagging tight ends, could dish out such warmth and empathy to a bunch of teenagers. She also kept telling them to be picky, not to settle, but to listen to their hearts. Was that what she was doing, listening to her heart, when she invited rock stars and who knew what else to stop by for a few rounds of bedtime bingo?

He shook his head. None of this matched up.

Putting aside the leather and the boots for a moment, could this beautiful person, the same one counseling seventeen-year-olds to follow their dreams, could *her* dream be to mow down more men than Al Capone on the way to a life spent...alone? All that intelligence and spirit wasted on a parade of nameless, faceless sex partners?

How sad.

"You're probably nuts," he told himself, earning him a glare from the young lady sitting in front of him. So he wrote down his thoughts instead of forming them out loud. *Okay, so I'm attracted to her. That's a given. Is that blinding me to who she really is? Or is it only the S&M outside and the sexual carousel that bothers me? And how much of it is a put-on? Which part?*

Is Nice Stevie the real one? Or Naughty?

As he considered what he knew about her, his hand stilled on the pen. His job was to see through pretense and decide who people really were. And if he let his instincts take over, adding up the innocent moan he'd replayed so many times on the tape recorder, the way she'd trembled under his hand in the bookstore and the tousled girl in the too-big robe this morning, he came up with a surprising picture of Stevie Bliss. Not a hard-edged, super-slick hottie, but a normal, vulnerable, living, breathing woman instead. A woman who was as attracted to him as he was to her, who didn't know how to handle it any better than he did.

What a mess.

"Underneath," he mused, "underneath the leather, I really believe there's someone very different hiding inside her. But how do I find that person?"

The girl in front of him turned around and made a hissing noise at him. "Could you be quiet, please?"

"Yeah, yeah." But Owen really felt he was on to something. Sure, she talked a good game, all about guarding your heart and playing around. Fun, fun, fun, 24/7. But when he listened to her, when she told the girls of the Brody Academy to hold on and hold out for someone who respected and cared for them, he saw something else.

He saw someone who still believed in love.

Suddenly, Owen knew what he had to do. The plan all along had been to follow her around for a day, right? So what if he changed the order of who was following whom?

What if he stole Stevie away from her set speeches and her patter and her faithful guard dog and dragged her out into the real world? Would the genuine inner Stevie come seeping out around the edges?

It was worth a try. At the very least, maybe he could satisfy some of his curiosity and stop driving himself crazy.

With a renewed sense of purpose, he noted Anna's location. As he tried to gauge how difficult it would be to head her off at the pass, Stevie asked for one final question, moving up the timetable.

He didn't know what he was going to do with her once he stole her away, but that was okay. He could improvise with the best of them. The important thing was to get her away from her controlled environment. Now.

Quickly, he slipped out of his seat, ducking out a side exit and reaching for his cell phone. A fast call to Anna, maybe some manufactured static and an urgent request for some info only she could provide....

STEVIE WAS A LITTLE SURPRISED. This was her first appearance in front of such a young crowd, and she hadn't been at all sure about how it would play. But Anna had arranged this as a personal favor for an old friend, who happened to be a counselor at the Brody Academy, which was, thank goodness, a pretty open and with-it kind of place. So they'd talked ahead of time about what subjects to stress and what to avoid. When she got there, she sort of went with the flow, putting away her notes and talking to the girls.

And it ended up feeling so natural and right. What a kick!

The kids were fabulous, even the teachers were getting into it, and better yet, she hadn't thought about Owen Dasher for hours. Well, okay, that wasn't true. As she spoke to the Brody girls, small, disturbing thoughts kept interfering, as if tiny pebbles had been tossed into the pool of her memory, creating larger ripples.

When she turned to take a question and her hair brushed her cheek, her brain reminded her that his fingers had been wound through that same hair.

When she took a step up the aisle, the soft leather of her skirt slid against her thigh, and she remembered with crystal clarity the moment his hand made the same journey.

When she leaned down to tug at the hem of her

skirt, her jacket gapped and her mind flashed to the image of her robe slipping apart, revealing more than she'd intended, and his fingers curving so close to her heart. Her own voice echoed in her ears. *What are you waiting for?*

Damn him, anyway. How could he be this much of a nuisance when he wasn't even there? And how could he keep invading her thoughts when her whole message was that she didn't need a man in the first place?

Well, I don't need him, she told herself. *I just want him. Which is a totally different thing.*

Staring into space, missing a question completely, she wondered again whether he would show up. With one eye on the entrance to the auditorium and so far, no sign of him, she was still unable to shake the feeling that he was lurking somewhere and would pop up when she least expected it.

It was strangely disappointing when he didn't. Maybe he'd been turned off by her ridiculous stories of Mr. December and football players and rock stars. She probably shouldn't have made that stuff up on the spur of the moment just to goad him.

Feeling gloomy, she shrugged. It really didn't matter, did it? So what if Owen was no longer interested in covering the Stevie Bliss story? She was much better off without him around to muddy up her Blissfully Single waters.

She saw Anna signal from the wings that she should wrap it up, so she asked for one more question, let another teen answer it herself and then thanked them all for their time.

She was shocked when they leapt to their feet to give her a standing ovation. Her—a standing O! It was so cool. She actually felt like a role model there for a second. And she wished Owen Dasher had been there to see it, which was a very strange thing to wish.

Stevie looked for Anna, not sure which way she was supposed to leave the auditorium. But where was Anna? That was odd. She'd been right behind the curtain a minute ago. Chewing the inside of her cheek, Stevie hesitated.

"Stevie? Can I speak to you privately?"

She held herself very still. The voice came from behind her, but she still knew it the instant she heard it. It had the familiar, melting effect, sending tingles down her spine, turning her into a puddle of warm goo, pitching her off balance and making her forget to breathe. Images tumbled through her mind, topsy-turvy, of his fingers in her hair, her robe slipping apart, his clever mouth so close to hers, his hand under her skirt...

He's here! she thought, bizarrely happy for a few seconds before her better judgment took over and squashed the silliness. *So what? So he showed up. Who cares?*

Determined to act nonchalant, she turned, clasping her hands tightly so she wouldn't be tempted to grab him or throw herself into his arms. Once again, he looked warm and pulled together, in the same clothes from this morning. He even had a scarf tossed over his coat, as if he'd just come in from the cold.

"Owen," she opened with, trying to sound unimpressed and not at all affected by his presence. She'd made a hash of things by letting him know how turned on she was the last time she saw him, and she wasn't going to let that happen again. This time, she had an advantage. She was completely dressed, with her Stevie Bliss persona firmly in place. Surely that would help. "I wasn't expecting you, but it's always nice to see you. When did you arrive?"

"I've been here the whole time," he said quickly, taking her by the arm and drawing her up the aisle. He seemed to be scanning the auditorium, looking over his shoulder for something or someone.

"What are you doing?" she inquired, glancing down at his hand under her elbow, so forcefully propelling her away from the stage. "What are *we* doing?"

He ignored the question. "I heard your speech." Holding open the door, he ushered her through. "You were great."

"Thank you. I think." She blinked. "But what is this all about? Why are you dragging me out of the auditorium?"

"I need to talk to you," he said impatiently. "Trust me. It's for your own good."

She stopped in her tracks, batting away his hand. "I don't respond well when people tell me something is for my own good."

"Yes, but this is."

"What is?" They were in the main hallway, outside some sort of trophy case. "What do you want to say?" she demanded. "And why couldn't you say it inside the auditorium?"

"It's a plot. A scheme. An escapade. Come on, we need to hurry." He tried to pull her along again, moving them toward the main entrance of the school, but she wasn't budging.

"What kind of escapade?" she asked suspiciously. None of this made any sense. He'd seen her speak to a bunch of teens and suddenly felt the need to launch a scheme to kidnap her? Huh?

"I needed to get you away from Anna. She's at the back door, waiting to meet what she thinks is a reporter from the *Tribune*, while we're at the front door, trying to escape," he explained calmly. "Oh, do you have another coat? Something to wear over that?"

"No, I don't wear a... Never mind." Stevie peered at him. "Owen, are you okay? Is there something wrong?" *Did I send you over the edge with all that crazy, made-up junk about my lovers?* Could someone as self-possessed as Owen turn into a stalker if provoked?

"I'm fine," he assured her. "And you will be, too. Once you come with me."

As she hesitated, he smiled, and it was so yummy it took her breath away. He really did have the most enchanting lips, with the bottom one a bit full in the middle and the top one narrow and elegant, with an upward curve at the corners that gave him just the hint of a dimple on one side. Lush. Sexy. Inviting. It made her want to dive right in.

But she couldn't think about that right now. "Why would I want to come away with you?" she asked warily.

"Oh, come on. You've never thought of playing hooky?"

"Playing hooky?" It only occurred to her every time she had to face a new group of protesting moms or another hour on the stationary bike. Or even make it through another afternoon without chocolate. How many times had she wanted to run away from it all?

"I like you, Stevie," he said softly, and her heart did a little dipsydoodle.

"Really? But I thought..." But she'd thought he was

disgusted by her sluttish résumé. Did he really like her?

"Would I say it if I didn't?" He shook his head. "I thought maybe you would enjoy a few hours away from the *Blissfully Single* rat race, when you didn't have to stay on message or worry about your image. A few daylight hours, I mean." His gaze narrowed. "I know your nights are full of fun and games."

"But I—"

"I realized," he interrupted, sounding a bit more caustic now, "that while you wrote about having fun and living life to the fullest, all you really do with your days is march from one appearance to the next, doing your duty, boring and dull, totally unlike the irreverent, spontaneous person you say you are." In a lighter tone, he continued, "I thought it would do you good to play hooky for one afternoon."

"Maybe. But I can't," she said regretfully. "I don't know where I'm supposed to be next, but Anna will have a fit—"

"Which is exactly why she's at the back door, waiting for a nonexistent reporter, while we sneak out the front." He took her by the lapels of her leather jacket and gazed directly into her eyes. "Dare to be different. Isn't that what you told the girls in there? You told them to face what scares them. Ditching your schedule scares you. *I* scare you. Face *me*, Stevie."

She gulped. Oh, God. He was so right. He did frighten her. If she'd had any pants, he would've scared them right off her. And there she was, advising all those impressionable seventeen-year-olds to seize hold of their fears and turn them into opportunities, while she was a scaredy-cat herself. She didn't know what to say.

"I looked at your schedule for this afternoon. There's nothing you can't do another time. And you know Anna will cover for you. Come on," he persuaded, back to that maddeningly charming voice he did so well. "You know what? It's officially the Christmas season. I'll bet you haven't been shopping for even one gift. And you're in Chicago, the best shopping town in the world."

Why did he have to be so adorable? She had no idea what his motives were, asking her along on this hooky-meets-shopping expedition, and she really didn't care. He was right. She'd been cooped up inside hotel rooms and health clubs and bookstores so long that she wasn't sure she could remember what the outside world looked like anymore.

She eyed him, noting his sweet smile and the sparkle in those sexy green eyes. Maybe he really did like her. Maybe he really did want to spend an afternoon with her. Was that so hard to believe?

After all, she was Stevie Bliss. Lots of men wanted to get next to her. Not usually for shopping, however.

"Just shopping?" she asked slowly. "This isn't a setup?"

"What kind of setup would it be?" he asked innocently. His smile widened. "You already told me it wasn't that hard to get into your pants. So why would I need a setup?"

Oh, yeah. What a tactic. Remind her of the ridiculous getting-into-my-pants crack. Not one of her finer moments. And then there were the other ones, where she'd practically begged him to kiss her. Yeah, she had really made a good impression so far, hadn't she?

She gazed into his eyes, and all she saw was a wonderful guy who seemed to want to spend a few hours with her. *Her.* Wasn't that what Stevie Bliss was all about? It wasn't easy to read and reread the book, to spread its message all the time, and not have any of the fun herself. As long as she was dressed and she kept him at arm's length, she was safe, wasn't she? She was hardly going to get into a situation where he had his hands on her, she melted at his touch, and he turned her down again. Perfectly safe. So what was she waiting for?

She made up her mind. "Okay."

"Okay?"

"I said okay, didn't I?"

"Stevie?" Anna's voice called out from behind her, back by the auditorium.

"Come on," Owen ordered, grabbing her hand, pulling her behind him.

"Stevie? Where are you going?"

But she ignored her friend's voice, scrambling to keep up with Owen in her high-heeled boots, whipping down the corridor, exulting in her chance to be wicked and reckless just this once. Wicked and reckless with Owen Dasher. It sounded pretty irresistible.

"Faster," she told him, enjoying her first rush of freedom. "I don't want Anna to catch us."

He grinned, and she knew he was caught up in the same reckless euphoria she was.

"Whoa," she cried, as they cleared the outside door and a cold blast of winter air hit her right in the face. "It's freezing out here!"

He turned back, blocking the wind as he tried to zip up her jacket. "You sure you don't have a coat?"

"This is my coat." Knocking his hands away, she zipped her own jacket. She was already shivering, and he wrapped an arm around her, hauling her down the stairs outside the school, hurrying her down the sidewalk. "My car's only a block away."

But one block felt like about six miles in this weather. So much for thinking their getaway escapade was fun. But as a fresh gust of icy wind knocked her into Owen and he tightened his grip, she laughed, burrowing in. Okay, it *was* fun.

The cold, bracing air made her realize she really was out on her own, without rules or restrictions. The day was hers, and she could do anything she wanted with it. What a marvelous idea.

She beamed at Owen. "I really ought to play hooky more often."

SO FAR, SO GOOD. Although he was improvising as he went, Stevie seemed happy with a mini-sightseeing tour, and no one was coming on to anyone. She was behaving like a normal person, not a sex kitten, and as long as he kept his eyes off her legs, he was doing okay too. It was working great.

"Where are we?" She craned her head up at the buildings. "What's this one?"

"It's the original Marshall Field's, built around the turn of the century. It's got character, don't you think?" He cupped one hand under her elbow, nudging her toward the doors. "I'll buy you some Frango mints. You'll love them."

"What's a Franco mint?"

"Not Franco. Frango. Chocolate mints. They're famous," he began, intending to explain quickly so he could point out the fabulous and intricately mechanized Christmas windows outside the store before they went in. But he stopped when he saw she'd already spotted the windows.

"Oh, wow." Leaving his side, Stevie ran to the second window, realized she'd missed one, and hurried back to catch the first. Her eyes were round with wonder. "This is incredible."

He trailed behind, enjoying the way she practically pressed her nose to the windows. They were spectacular, and his nieces loved them. Every year they made a family expedition down to see Marshall Field's windows, and they had since before he was born. But he hadn't been sure Stevie would really be that interested.

"Look, Owen, did you see this?" she asked, in a hushed, awe-filled tone. "It's *A Christmas Carol*. They all move. Down to the tiniest thing. Scrooge is in the counting house in the first one, and there's Tiny Tim. Don't you love Tiny Tim? Look at the little crutches. Oh, my God! He takes a few steps on the tiny crutches and then his dad swings him up on his shoulder. It's amazing!"

"I'm glad you like it," he said with amusement.

"And over here, there's the Ghost of Christmas Past and Belle and Mr. Fezziwig. They're dancing! And look, here, with the whole Cratchit family around the table with the big goose. Look, they're smiling, and Bob Cratchit carves the goose. Oh, wow. I've never seen anything so..."

Her voice seemed to crack, and Owen blinked. Were those tears welling up behind her snappy little glasses? Sure, the elaborate Christmas windows were beautiful. But why would they make Stevie cry?

"You've never seen anything so...what?" he prompted, trying to get a handle on what was happening here.

"So sweet," she whispered, tracing one finger

against the glass. "I've seen the Alastair Sims movie so many times. And yet I forget sometimes how sentimental Christmas can be when you go all Dickens on it. You know, second chances, family, sharing. God bless us, every one."

"Are you okay?" he asked softly, not sure what to do. He'd wanted to see the real Stevie, but he hadn't expected to open up the floodgates.

"Sure, sure. I'm fine. Just fine." She wiped her eyes quickly, pushed up her glasses, and turned back to him. Her smile was bright, if a shade forced, and she shivered. "Must be the cold making my eyes water."

Yeah, right. As he led the way into the store, he pondered this interesting turn of events. So sultry Stevie Bliss knew every character from *A Christmas Carol*, and she got all choked up over Christmas windows. *Second chances, family, sharing...*

Talk about cracks in the facade.

6

AFTER SHE'D MADE an idiot of herself over the Marshall Field's Christmas windows, Owen shepherded her inside the store.

"What would you like to look at first? Who's on your list?" he asked.

"My list? But I don't..." Feeling wounded, she broke off.

Okay, Stevie. Straighten up and fly right. First she'd gotten all weepy up over some stupid windows, and now she felt like he'd shot her when he'd simply asked who she exchanged Christmas gifts with. She felt like an orphan child, right out of *Oliver Twist*, which was Dickens, but not the right Dickens. It was ridiculous.

So what if she had no one on her Christmas list? Except Anna, of course. The two of them always managed to exchange tasteful organizers or expensive fountain pens ordered out of some in-flight catalog. They were too busy to shop. There were three- and five-year plans to plot out, decisions to make, numbers to crunch, surveys to draft. It had been that way for several years, and it hadn't bothered her then, had it?

Well, actually, it had. The holidays always gave her the willies, if she were honest. And being smack in the middle of this grand old department store, with

Christmas staring her right in the face from every brimming counter and overflowing display, her willies were blowing themselves into a full-blown panic attack.

Christmas list? she wanted to shout. *I spit on Christmas lists! I'm way too cool for Christmas lists.*

Except she didn't. And she wasn't.

Besides, she knew Owen was just trying to be nice. If he'd made a habit of coming on like gangbusters before, teasing her with frank talk and too many almost-kisses, now he was treating her like something from the "You break it, you buy it" shelf.

All because she'd sniffled a little. Sheesh. Men and tears. What a bunch of wussies. She actually preferred the snotty, sarcastic Owen to this one with the soft eyes and uncertain look on his face. *Men.* When you couldn't even trust them to be mean and selfish, what was the world coming to?

"Stevie, are you okay?" he asked one more time, the picture of concern.

"I'm fine. It's just that I..." Thinking quickly, she told him, "I realized that I didn't bring a purse. No money or credit cards. Not even an ATM card. So no shopping for me today."

"You don't want to shop?" he asked slowly, making her feel as if she were letting down not only him, but all of womanhood and consumerhood in one fell swoop. "I could float you a loan. I mean, it's not like I don't know where to find you if you don't pay me back."

Leave it to Owen. He didn't make things easy, did he? She mumbled, "No, really. I've already done most of my shopping, anyway, so I'm good."

"What about souvenirs to bring home from Chicago?" he asked. "How about some Frango mints?"

"We don't eat those in my, uh, family," she said quickly, wondering what the deal was with Owen and those mints. "Not big on candy."

"Here they are." Heading for a tall display, piled with dark green boxes that smelled pretty good even wrapped up, he confessed, "I give out a lot of these."

She took a gander at the number of boxes he was carrying and murmured, "Yeah, I guess so. Is that your whole list?"

"Not even close. I've got my mom, my sisters, their husbands, their kids. Let's see... Among my four sisters, I have six nieces."

"Four sisters?" she echoed. "And six nieces? All girls?"

No wonder he knew how to wrap women around his little finger. His personal life was oozing with girls.

"Are they all in the area?" she inquired, wondering who might come leaping out from the accessories aisle, demanding to know what the hussy was doing shopping with her brother.

"Yep. A few in the suburbs, but still close. Born and bred in Chicago, you know, so we don't stray far." He grinned. "My mom's still mad at me for working for the *Chronicle*. She's a *Sun-Times* kind of woman. Plus I've written a few stories on the Cubs, and she's a dyed-in-the-wool White Sox fan. Never the twain shall meet, you know?"

She had no idea what he was talking about, but she got the underlying idea. Mom. Sisters. Family with a capital *F*, all very involved in his life. "Very *Life With Father*," she said out loud.

"What's that?"

"Nothing." For her, that would've been awful, to have so many relatives poking over what she did and said. One of the reasons Stephanie Blanton could disappear and Stevie Bliss take her place was that no one would really notice she was missing. But Owen... Owen had people who noticed everything, it seemed.

"So," she ventured, "it sounds like you see them pretty often. Holidays and all that."

"Actually, yeah. I do."

"That's...lovely," she offered. There had been a time when she'd dreamt of noisy family Christmas dinners, very much like the one the Cratchit family was having in an eternal loop outside in the windows. But she'd thought she was past that. She'd thought turning into Stevie Bliss had catapulted her past mushy family junk and into some kind of much more sensible no strings/no connections person. So why was she poking into this? "And where do you fit in?"

"I'm the youngest, actually."

The youngest and the only son. Adored, protected and spoiled, no doubt. It just kept getting worse. A woman would be insane to go near Owen with that kind of rear guard.

"I think you're really lucky," she managed, trailing behind as he went up to the counter to pay for the chocolates. "To have all that family, and to be close, I mean. Not many people have that."

"I know. But it gets tough when you're trying to buy gifts. Besides, I hate shopping," he admitted. "My sisters and even my mom, I go with wall-to-wall gift certificates, but the kids..." The clerk handed him back his card and his purchases, and when he turned to Stevie, he was toting a large shopping bag full of chocolates. "Who knows what to pick out for a bunch of little girls? I'm lost. Although you could take pity on me and pitch in."

"Excuse me?" He wanted *her* to help choose gifts? This sounded way over her head. Unless they were in her target demographic, and she very much doubted that Owen had nieces over 18, she didn't have any hard information to deal with. She allowed, "I don't think I'd be much help."

"Oh, come on. You were a little girl once." With his free hand, he nabbed a talking Christmas tree toy off a special display and squeezed it, making it jiggle its little branches and belch out something in the area of "Ho ho ho." Owen held it out. "Would you have wanted this?"

"Uh, no."

"See? I knew you'd know what to buy."

"I didn't say that. I said I wouldn't have wanted that. But it might've been perfect for someone else." Although when it came to the talking Christmas tree, she doubted it.

"Please? Come on. Help me out here."

She frowned, giving the bustling store a good look, testing herself, automatically dividing merchandise into *hot* and *not hot* in her mind. Huh. It wasn't hard to tell, actually. Even without market surveys or focus groups, she still knew that the gaudy Christmas tote bags were good for grandmas while the dangly, lighted earrings would play to the kid crowd, that they shouldn't waste their time marketing the "Auld Lang Syne" jewelry boxes to anyone under fifty or the glittery makeup kits to anyone over twelve. Musing as she surveyed the array of merchandise, she asked,

"How old did you say your nieces were? And how much do you want to spend?"

"The oldest is eleven and the youngest is seven." His words were rushed, as if he wanted to get her working on this before she changed her mind. "Oh, and I don't care what I spend. I'm their uncle. I'm supposed to spoil them." And he winked at her.

Great wink. It made her wish that she was eleven again and he could be her uncle. But no. That left out way too many fun possibilities. But, sheesh. To be a kid with a devoted uncle with an unlimited budget. What a kick.

"Six nieces between the ages of seven and eleven?" she asked. "Your sisters must've been busy all at the same time."

"They're competitive. One started and the others all tried to keep up." He began to make his way to the escalator under a sky-lighted atrium. "Come on. The toy department is upstairs."

But Stevie held back. Suddenly, she knew exactly what the 7-to-11 demographic would want for Christmas, and it wasn't in the toy department. "You don't really want toys, do you?"

"Don't I?"

"No," she stated with sudden certainty. "You need to go with clothes and cosmetics."

Owen hesitated. "You think so?"

Hands on her hips, she gave him a level stare. It was kind of fun to be the expert, to be leading Owen Dasher around by the nose. And when it came to consumer products, she *was* an expert. Maybe not for this exact age group, but close enough. "You were the one who said I should know what they like. Well, you were right. I know exactly what girls want."

This girl wanted an afternoon with Owen Dasher, where she could impress him with her wit and charm and sweep him off his feet. But he didn't have to know that. Heck, she hadn't even known that herself till just this minute.

He shrugged. "Okay. Lead the way."

"Here." Dragging him across the aisle into jewelry, she snagged half a dozen packs of stick-on jewelry that came in various colors and designs. "You can stick these on as a necklace or a bracelet, or like a tattoo on your arm or your back, so if you wear a skimpy top, the whole jewel pattern will show," she explained. "They'll love them. Oh, and those, over there."

Pulling him along to the cosmetics department, she picked out six makeup kits in shades of pink and purple, handing them over one at a time. "What are these?" he asked, trying to juggle his Frango bag enough to get a look at what she was giving him.

"Makeup. Just right for preteens since it's all glittery stuff." She flipped open a lid to show him. "They have all the brushes and applicators as well as body paint, blush, eye shadow and lipstick in fun flavors, like, uh, strawberry. Perfect."

Owen didn't look convinced.

"Trust me," she told him.

She hadn't really considered the implications of that statement, but she could tell Owen did. As he gazed at her, she could see the wheels spinning inside his gorgeous head. "You know, Stevie, it's the weirdest thing. I do trust you."

Uh-oh. She was starting to feel warm and runny again. First he liked her and now he trusted her. What next? She chewed her lip. Maybe she didn't want to go there. Maybe if she did, she'd be ripping off her clothes and asking him to make love to her, right there in front of the Clinique counter.

Every time she was around him for more than five minutes, it seemed to come back to sex. And she was determined not to let it. Not this time.

"I..." But she didn't know how to finish that. "I think the makeup kits will be a big hit," she managed. "And if you're really on an unlimited budget, after this, let's look at clothes, okay?"

He smiled. "I am completely in your hands."

That sounded very good to her. Too good.

But he took a step backward, toward the counter. "I'll just, uh, pay for what we've collected so far."

Thank you, God or Goddess, or whoever was sending him away long enough for her to catch her breath. "I'm going to the girls department," she called out, purposely not looking at him as she raced through the atrium to the escalator. It wasn't like there was a time limit, and yet she felt as if she had to rush, mostly just to get away from Owen and the possibility of him being completely in her hands.

As the escalator wound its way up, she told herself that her frayed nerves and frantic pace had nothing to do with Owen, after all. No, it was just because this afternoon hooky session was so unexpected, so out of the normal routine. And time was wearing on, too, while Anna was undoubtedly wondering where she'd gotten off to.

"I didn't even tell her how long I would be gone," she muttered. Poor Anna was probably still on the phone, rearranging appointments and cursing Stevie's name. Or Stephanie's.

But, no. This was a Stevie problem. Stephanie the

responsible would never have run away from an obligation. Whereas Stevie was unreliable, self-absorbed and unreasonable. She did what she wanted, when she wanted. Damn the consequences, full speed ahead. Which, if you started putting Owen into the mix, could be a pretty dangerous cocktail.

"It's her fault," Stevie said out loud as she hit the fifth floor, which was clearly the children's department. She entered the area under a giant train, bypassing the line to see Santa, heading for girls' clothes instead. "She's the one who told me to *live* the part, not just play it."

And a department store like this was a pretty great place to start, too. Wide-eyed, thrilled, she realized this was getting better by the minute. Too busy with her packed schedule of appearances, she never got to do stuff like roam a few stores. And especially not to browse fun stuff like tiny fleece miniskirts with matching Lycra crop tops. Oooh, and matching fuzzy go-go boots, too!

"Every girl is going to want those," the saleswoman said brightly. "Did you see the matching earmuffs? And backpacks?"

"I know!" Stevie enthused, holding up a tiger-striped miniskirt. Did she like the zebra or the tiger print better? And what about the leopard one, with spots? Too adorable for words. "It might be worth having kids if you could dress them like this."

"What?"

That was Owen's voice. She wheeled around. He'd arrived with all his parcels and bags and her heart did its usual thumper routine. If only he would stop sneaking up on her. Yeah, sure, it was the sneaking that was the problem.

She brandished the tiger skirt and a pair of earmuffs. "Aren't these wonderful?"

"Well, I don't know. Are they?"

"Everything matches," she told him, trying to stress just how ideal these gifts were. "Skirts, tops, boots, earmuffs and even backpacks. All in jungle prints. Everything but the tops are furry, see? Kids love furry. And look, they come in zebra or tiger or leopard. This stuff is to die for."

"Okay," he said doubtfully, poking at the fleece as if he thought it might bite. "Well, at least you're a quick shopper."

"What sizes do you think?"

"I don't know." He shrugged. "Normal."

Men. Shopping for children whose sizes they didn't know. How did they manage to survive when they were so clueless? No wonder they needed women in their lives so badly. "Slim? Or chunky? Tall? Short?"

"Just normal," he said again.

"Okay, well, we'll buy the sizes based on their ages, and they can always exchange them if they don't fit. Okay?"

"Sure."

Busying herself with earmuffs and backpacks was a good way not to think about him and what he smelled like and how his eyes twinkled that way and how his dimple peeked out when she least expected it. She patiently found the right sizes as he told her how old each child was. Feeling more than a little spaced out, she piled all their items on the counter, rechecking to be sure she had six of everything, all in the right sizes and patterns. Although she was normally a details person, it was all a blur at this point.

"Stevie, I really appreciate this," Owen offered. "I

never would've bought any of this stuff without you. My poor nieces would be getting teddy bears for the tenth year in a row, I'm afraid."

"It's okay," she returned, feeling more than a little awkward. She had been useful to Owen. He was grateful. It was kind of cool, actually. "I'm enjoying it."

"I'd really like to thank you. What do you say I get you something?"

A gift? For her? When Christmas rolled around, she was used to a new wallet or a belt from Anna and that was it. "That's so sweet of you," she whispered.

But then she remembered who exactly he thought she was. Considering what he'd written in his column, she could just imagine what he'd come up with for a thank you gift. Slinky lingerie. Sex toys. Maybe a whip. She spun around, almost knocking little jungle print separates all over the floor. "No thank-you present necessary," she said quickly.

"No, no, I'm serious." He took her arm as the saleslady began to box up the children's clothes. "Something warm maybe. What you're wearing..." His gaze swept her from head to toe as he fingered the leather of her jacket. "You have to be freezing. Think about it. Wouldn't some warm clothes be nice? You can change right here, before we leave."

Stevie stiffened. Something warm? Good grief. That wasn't at all what she'd figured he'd go for. "Like what?"

"I saw these great sweaters, really bulky and thick, and maybe some jeans or corduroys. I know you'd love them. Baggy, comfortable, you know."

A sweater and jeans? For Stevie Bliss? She looked down at her short leather skirt and boots, her tight-fitting leather jacket. Yes, she was freezing. Her carefully choreographed persona did not take into account the fact that breezes shot under her skirt and down her front and that there was bare skin between her knees and her hem. But a *sweater? Jeans?*

She was willing to be flexible enough to ditch Anna and run away for one afternoon, but not to give up her whole identity. How would she know how to behave in regular clothes? Who would she be? She started to panic again just considering facing the world—facing Owen—without the Stevie Bliss trappings.

"That doesn't really sound like me," she tried. She managed a hollow laugh. "What would my fans think if they saw me running around in a bulky sweater and baggy jeans?"

"Maybe," he said, leaning in closer, "that it was winter in Chicago and you wanted to stay warm?"

She edged away. "Thank you, but I don't think so."

Her mind was racing with this new turn of events. *Why doesn't he like the way I dress? Why does he want to cover me up?* It wasn't very flattering, was it?

Okay, so she was offended to think he wanted to buy her something erotic, and then equally offended when he went for the total opposite. A lot of men bought woman sweaters. It didn't mean anything, just that he was the usual clueless male when it came to gifts. There was no point getting all bent out of shape about it, especially when she'd been miffed about the other side of the coin, too.

Better decide what you want, Stevie, she told herself. *Do you want him to look at you as a sex object? Or do you want him to throw sweaters and coats and blankets at you so he can think of you as his pal?* Was either satisfactory?

Under her breath, she murmured, "Maybe I want both."

"You change your mind about the sweater and jeans?"

"Um, no, I was thinking about something else."

"All right, if you don't want the warm clothes," he put in kindly, "can we at least look in the lingerie department? Maybe we can find a gift there."

She was strangely cheered by that thought. This was more what she'd been thinking. A teddy, a slinky chemise, something sinful. It wasn't what she really wore to bed or anywhere else, but at least he was in the same ballpark as everyone else who tried to buy her favors. He *was* attracted to her. He liked her, he trusted her and he wanted her. Or at least he wanted to buy lingerie for her.

"Well, we can look, anyway," she decided.

"Good."

So she grabbed the bag of neatly boxed jungle-print clothes, and followed Owen as he tried to find a path through crowds of shoppers and strollers and stacked displays. Business in the store had really picked up just since they got there. Or maybe it was so crowded because they were close to Santa and the line of children curving around and around, waiting to see Jolly Old St. Nick. Owen was really good at finding holes in the traffic, even with so many bags, while Stevie did her best to keep up. But she wasn't as skillful at the dodge-and-dart game as he was.

"Excuse me," she said more than once, as she tried to cut through the line to pass to the other side. But then she got stuck completely when a very short man in a goofy green suit planted himself right in her path. He had to be under five-five, and he wore a funny stocking cap, striped stockings and curly-toed shoes, all bright green. One of Santa's elves? Whatever he was supposed to be, he was leering at her.

"Hey, lady, you wanna sit on Santa's knee?" he asked, giving her the eye, up and down and back again. "I can get you to the front of the line. Or better yet, you can come play in the candy cane house out back, huh?"

She was so surprised she didn't know what to say for a second. This was the first time she'd ever been accosted by an elf. "Do you work here?" she got out after a long moment, as she stared down at him. If he was wearing an elf suit and he didn't work there, they were all in trouble.

"I'm on break."

"I don't care," she started. "I really don't think you're supposed to be hitting on people while—"

"Aw, don't get all bent out of shape," he interrupted. "It's a compliment. You're hot. Just 'cause I'm an elf, I'm not allowed to say something to a hot chick?"

"Mommy, that lady is being mean to the elf," a nearby child said loudly.

Stevie turned quickly, accidentally smacking the elf with her bag. "I wasn't being mean to him," she explained. "He was being rude—"

But her words were drowned out by the same unhappy girl, who began to wail at the top of her lungs. "She hit Santa's elf! She hit Santa's elf!" She sure was making a lot of noise for someone that small. Unfortunately, her clarion call started a chain reaction down the line, as child after child began to shriek and howl. Stevie was relatively sure it wasn't her fault—probably just a case of cranky children who'd been in line too long—but she still didn't know what to do.

"Please don't cry," she tried, as the elf forcefully pinched her butt from behind. She spun around, dropping her bag. "Stop that!"

Screaming children, a grabby elf, too many people and nowhere to run! It was Christmas Hell.

And suddenly, there was Owen. "I wondered where you'd wandered off to," he said calmly, picking up the shopping bag she'd dropped and adding it to his own load. Then he loomed over the small man in the elf outfit. "You. Leave the lady alone."

"I wasn't..." the elf began, but his words trailed off when he caught the look on Owen's face.

Very impressive. She hadn't really seen him do a full-scale glower before. There was something to be said for White Knights who appeared out of nowhere, just when you needed them to save you from evil elves.

"Thank you," she murmured, sliding closer, out of elf range. Now if only he could do something about all the crying kiddies.

"Let's get out of here," Owen whispered into her ear, leaning in close enough to ruffle her hair with his warm breath.

She wanted to lean right back, wrapping herself around him until she blocked out the rest of the melee. She didn't. "How?"

"I think they'll get tired of screaming eventually, but I don't plan to wait long enough to find out," he announced, already clearing a path, waiting for her to go first. "So here's the deal. Stay with me. If we get separated, go down the wide aisle past the escalator and hook left. Ladies lingerie, dead ahead, under the famous Tiffany ceiling. I already scoped it out."

She was stuck to him like glue, since she had no intention of loitering anywhere near the Santa line.

It took a few minutes to navigate, but she knew she was in the right place when she saw the sparkling ceiling. Wow. And then there was a mannequin draped in a short, skimpy cream-colored chemise. And a very pretty chemise it was, too, with two narrow bands of red ribbon, one cinched under the bodice and the other sliding down the right side from the strap to the hem. Where the ribbons intersected, there was a delicate red bow and a tag that said Open Me First, as if to indicate that the lady who wore it was the gift all by herself.

Very cute. She sent him a quick glance, trying to telegraph that this item would be an excellent choice, if he still wanted to buy her something.

But Owen swept past the mannequin in the gift-wrapped chemise, heading for a table full of...

Underwear? And not sassy bikinis or thongs, either. The piles of underpants on the table were big, fat, hideous cotton briefs, three for fifteen dollars. The kind everyone's grandma wore. The kind she and a college roommate had dubbed "icky pants" when they saw them in a basket in the dorm laundry room.

Was this a joke? She was so surprised she started to laugh.

"You're not serious, are you?" she said when she caught her breath. He wasn't laughing. "But I don't wear underwear at all, let alone those."

"I know. Maybe you should start?"

"Maybe I should...?" Her eyes widened. First bulky

sweaters and now the stodgiest of stodgy underpants? What was this all about?

"Never mind," he mumbled. Oh, man. He *was* serious. But he had clearly caught the disbelief written on her face, and he was backtracking. Or backtracking as much as a steamroller could. "Listen, I saw something I wanted for one of my sisters a few floors down. You look at whatever you want, maybe think about the underwear thing. Who knows? Come get me if you change your mind and you need me to pay. Or whatever. I'll, uh, meet you down by the chocolate display where we came in, okay?"

"Owen..." But he was already gone. He had offered a gift. She had obviously not appreciated said gift, he picked up on the lack of appreciation, and now she felt guilty. And after he'd saved her from the elf, too. On the other hand...

She wanted to swear. She wanted to trash the hideous underpants display and throw a tantrum right there. *I don't get him!* she thought, not for the first time.

But this time, she felt perfectly justified. Who would ever understand a man who took you to the lingerie department and then wanted to buy icky pants?

She frowned at the table. There was absolutely no way this made sense. Unless...

"Unless he's trying to reform my evil ways," she said out loud. Oh, yeah. It fit. Sweaters and jeans and plain cotton underpants. Turning Stevie Bliss back into Stephanie Blanton, the woman he never would've looked at twice. Except even Stephanie Blanton wouldn't wear those awful things.

"Men are all nuts," she decided. "They *so* don't know what they want."

She, however, knew what she wanted. Besides

Owen. Or at least a version of Owen who made sense occasionally.

She unzipped her jacket, feeling for the tiny inside pocket where she always kept an American Express card to use in case of emergency. Did this constitute an emergency? You bet it did.

She wanted that slinky cream-colored chemise, the one with the red ribbons and the Open Me First tag. She wanted it bad. She told herself it might come in handy if Owen decided to drop by her suite again unexpectedly.

Lifting her chin, Stevie found the rack with the gown she wanted, grabbed her size and marched over to the register.

"Is this a gift?" the clerk asked.

"No. It's for me. Absolutely, positively for *me*."

And if she opened the door wearing nothing but this thing, she guaranteed he wouldn't waste time trying to change her into someone else.

7

OWEN WAS positively laden down with shopping bags when she found him near the Frango mint display, and he looked just about as grumpy as any man would in that position.

She was still feeling a little snippy about the underpants debacle, and she asked, rather crisply, "Did you find what you wanted?"

He mumbled something noncommittal, but she did catch, "I really need to get out of here before my head explodes," or something like that. Fear of shopping. It got them every time.

"Owen, why did you bring me here when you obviously hate to shop?" she asked, not quite keeping the edge out of her voice.

"I don't hate it." He considered. "Okay, I do hate it. But I thought you would enjoy it. Marshall Field's is a Chicago institution, and you hadn't really seen anything of the city yet except a few bookstores and the inside of one high school. It's my town, you know." He shrugged, offering a wry smile that made her want to kiss him. It wasn't hard. Everything made her want to kiss him. "Next up—the Billy Goat Tavern."

"That doesn't sound good," she said slowly. "Do they serve goat or something?"

"I don't think so. But you never know." He glanced around, moving himself and his packages aside barely in time to avoid a woman with a stroller. "Can we get out of here, please?"

She made a step in that direction and then hastily pulled back as a crowd of teenage girls came barreling through on their way to the cosmetic counter. "I'm trying. There's not a whole lot of room to maneuver here." Not unless she wanted to leap over his bags or carry her own over her head.

His eyes narrowed on the heavy shopping bag she was lugging behind her. It wasn't that she was hiding it. But she also wasn't advertising it. After she'd bought the chemise, she'd practically tripped over a pair of extremely expensive and wickedly cute red boots in the shoe department, and she couldn't resist. They were in a large box, which barely fit inside the largest handled shopping bag available. She wanted to show him her purchases. *Do you see, Owen? Snappy lingerie and hot little red boots are right for me, while icky pants are not!* But she refrained. He'd suffered enough. And he had saved her from the elf.

"I thought you couldn't buy anything," he reminded her. "I thought you didn't have any money."

Damn, the man was sharp. "I found some cash in my pocket." *Stevie, Stevie.* Dishonesty had become her middle name.

"That seems unlikely," he grumbled.

"What do you think, I shoplifted?" She shook her head, taking her opening and her new boots and beating a self-righteous path to the front door. Okay, so she was lying. She didn't even know why she was lying at this point. She could just as easily have said she'd found the credit card in her pocket. Habit, apparently.

"I don't suppose you bought yourself a winter coat?" he asked. "Scarf? Hat? Mittens?"

"You are really flogging that one, aren't you? I told you, I don't need any of that."

But Owen's expression told her he didn't believe her. He reached into one of his bags, rummaging around for a second or two before he emerged with a pair of black earmuffs and some fuzzy black mittens.

"For me?"

Without comment, he flipped them over to her, making her drop her bag with a clatter in order to catch them.

She considered refusing the gift. But she wasn't stupid. She kept her mouth shut, ripping off the tags, jamming her hands into the mittens and carefully settling the earmuffs on over her hair.

With a mocking lift of one eyebrow, Owen held the door open for her without further comment. She stepped out into the winter sidewalk scene, greeted immediately by a blast of cold air and a teeth-rattling chill that made her want to smack him for being right. Maybe she should've bent her pride and taken him up on the sweater, too. Or even the underpants. Wearing so little clothing, with wind whipping right up her skirt, was totally dopey, wasn't it? She had one frozen bootie, and all in the name of the Stevie Bliss image. She shivered.

Moving quickly, hugging her shopping bag in front of her as a wind break, she pulled to a stop as Owen stuffed a few bills into a bell-ringer's charity cauldron. Behind the bell-ringer, somebody sang an off-key version of "Santa Claus is Coming to Town."

Oh, great. She really needed to hear about being good for goodness sake. Lying, running away, buying lingerie in the faint hope that Owen would want to take it off her later... Not good. On the other hand, she hadn't pouted yet. So maybe there was some chance Santa would still reward her. Perhaps by sending Owen over to catch her in the gift-wrapped nightie.

"You better watch out," the wretched singer blared at her, as if he knew she was the baddest girl on the block.

She realized glaring at the singer would not have shown the proper holiday spirit, but she was still considering it when another group of pedestrians caught her eye.

"Owen, look!" A young woman with a stroller had just turned the corner. The baby strapped into the stroller was well-covered, but also festive, bundled into a reindeer suit, complete with antlers attached to the top of his hood and a red foam ball fastened over his tiny button nose. "Isn't that cute?"

"I think you should stay away from people in Christmas costumes. The elf was kind of a disaster," Owen said dryly.

"This is a baby," she returned. "Unlikely to pinch my bottom."

Owen's tone was grim when he responded, "You never know. Depends on whether it's a boy."

"Besides, the elf altercation wasn't my fault," she went on, ignoring him. "They should fire the little weasel. And they shouldn't keep children waiting so long in line, either. That's why they all started to cry. I didn't do anything."

But the reindeer baby had rolled closer by now, and Stevie broke away from Owen, unable to resist gushing a little bit. "What a sweet little outfit," she cried, bending down, pulling off one mitten with her teeth, and then tweaking his antlers and his funny red nose. He gurgled happily.

His mother grinned. "It keeps his nose warm, too."

"He's adorable." She wanted to hold him, but she couldn't really ask to take him out of the stroller when he was all strapped in like that. So she leaned in closer, tickling his chin as he watched her, wide-eyed. He kicked his tiny legs, staring up at her with the joy of total innocence.

"I think he likes you," his mom offered. "Either that or he has gas."

But the baby curled his whole tiny hand, safe inside a mitten, around one of her fingers. Awesome. She swallowed, feeling her eyes mist over for the second time today. Jiggling his hand, she cooed, "You're Santa's cutest little reindeer, aren't you?"

Still on the baby's level, she straightened enough to note Owen's reaction to all this. As he stood back, observing every detail, she realized his expression was as serious and watchful as the baby in the stroller. She disentangled her finger, rising, pulling away, shoving her hand back into her mitten.

The baby's mother pushed on, waving goodbye and calling out, "Merry Christmas!"

"To you, too," Stevie murmured.

Owen's gaze remained bemused and thoughtful.

"What?" she asked, rejoining him. "He was cute, okay? And you could have one like him someday, you know. I mean, if I had your baby, I'd probably be putting him in reindeer suits year-round."

He seemed taken aback at that one, and she replayed what she'd said. *If I had your baby...*

Okay, this was awful. Very, very awful.

Trying to extricate herself, she rushed to add, "Because your name is Dasher, I mean. Dasher. Reindeer. Get it?"

"I got it." But a hint of a smile played around his lips. "Lame joke."

"Yeah, you probably get a lot of that this time of year, don't you? Sorry. I didn't mean anything by it," she assured him. "I have some trouble... I mean, I shouldn't have..."

"It's okay. It was kind of cute."

Cute was not what she was looking for. But she'd take it if it meant they never had to discuss the *If I had your baby* concept ever again.

She took his arm, hoisting her bag in her other hand so it didn't knock into his. Latching on to him like that was probably cozier than she wanted to be, but she couldn't help it. For one thing, she felt like a Popsicle. She wondered if those were really ice crystals attaching themselves to her thighs.

For another, he was incredibly sweet, and this whole day had been so strange and unsettling, she needed someone to hold on to. It felt right, in a solid, steady way, to be strolling down the sidewalk with him, passing carolers and bell-ringers, arms entwined, as if they were a... A couple.

Uh-oh. Dangerous turf. And yet par for the course with the day she'd had. So far, she'd come on to him wearing nothing but a robe and been turned down flat, wowed a crowd of teenagers, agreed to run off and play hooky for the first time in her life, gotten choked up over a window display and her lack of a shopping list, picked fights over underpants and elves, gushed all over someone else's baby, made mention of having *his* baby and in general, acted like an emotional mushball. He must think she was nuttier than a fruitcake.

She tried to explain, "There's just something about Christmas that gets to me. I start to feel, I don't know, kind of wistful and sentimental." She lifted her shoulders in a shrug, digging herself a deeper hole. "I think a lot of people are in the same boat at this time of year, don't you? Seasonal weirdness?"

"Seasonal affective disorder," he supplied.

"Exactly. Well, not exactly. That's about the weather, right? Or sunshine?" Thinking out loud, she added, "For me, it's totally the holidays themselves. All the togetherness and good cheer. It almost makes it worse to know it was my own choice. It's true that Anna colluded, but I have to take responsibility, too. I'm the one who decided to give up any right to this kind of stuff when I..."

She broke off. She could tell by the look of avid interest on his face that she was offering too much information.

He was gazing at her as if he could see right through her, all the way down to some deep-seated need to abandon all of her *Blissfully Single* principles and become one more teary housefrau rocking a cradle full of tiny reindeer, bargaining away her freedom just so there would be someone to unwrap packages with on Christmas morning.

What a mess. And it was all Christmas's fault. She was perfectly happy and logical and sensible the rest of the year!

"Never mind," she said slowly. But he was still looking at her, not saying anything, just looking, all soft and tender, as if she'd turned into an angel right before his eyes.

Unlikely.

She dipped her gaze, not really ready to be looked at like that. "What next?" she inquired, trying to think of something casual to say. "Billy Goat Tavern?"

"That's pretty much up to you." He unlocked the car, opening her door and then heading back around to load up the trunk with their parcels. "More hooky? Or back to the grind?"

She ducked in quickly while he was otherwise occupied. Her difficulty getting in and out of cars without flashing the world was one more thing Anna hadn't thought through. Sure, the focus groups loved the idea of no underwear, but had they ever tried levering themselves into the front seat of a low-slung car in a short skirt without panties?

Stevie sat there, tugging her skirt down as close to her knees as she could get, wondering what she should choose. Head back to the Hotel Marceau and face Anna and the consequences of this afternoon on the lam? Or prolong the escapade a little longer?

No contest. "As long as you turn up the heat in here," she said, hugging herself, rubbing her mittened hands over her arms, "I'm game for another adventure."

Owen cranked the heater up as high as it would go. "Told you to take a sweater."

"Yeah, yeah, yeah." She glared at him. With spirit, she added, "No one likes a know-it-all."

But Owen laughed out loud. Still not pulling away from the curb, he sent her another glance. "Stevie, you really are something else."

"You said that before," she said, tugging off her mittens and splaying her fingers in front of the heater vent. The air was cold, but it was still warmer than she was. "The first time, I think you meant it in a bad way. This time..." She let her own gaze dart over to his. "This time, I think you mean it in a good way. Right?"

He continued to shake his head. "I really don't know what to do with you. But I have an idea."

She had an idea what to do with him, as well. Something about a roaring fire, a furry rug and a lot of sweat and bare skin. Better keep that one to herself.

"Come on," he said, switching off the car and opening his door. "I know where I want to take you."

"Outside? Again?" she asked doubtfully. "I was just starting to defrost."

"It isn't far. We'll walk fast."

His idea turned out to be not a tavern, Billy Goat or otherwise, but instead a skating rink. Which was, of course, pretty much the polar opposite of her roaring fire and bare skin.

"Why a skating rink?" she inquired, looking around at the wide expanse of ice. As a cold, cloudy darkness began to fall, there was a scattering of skaters under a few strings of Christmas lights, in the midst of a large park carved right into the middle of the city. If not exactly Currier and Ives, it was still atmospheric.

"It's called winter fun. Ever heard of it?" he asked in a sardonic tone.

"I'm not much into outside winter fun. I don't think I've ever ice-skated before." She looked down at her boots and their three-inch heels, deciding to hang on to Owen a bit tighter as they neared the rink. Even being close to that much ice made her afraid she was going to go splat and make a fool of herself. Not to mention risking exposing her tangled limbs and bare bottom to the entire world. Or at least a few skaters.

"Not a lot of ice-skating in Samoa, huh?"

"Samoa? Why would...? Oh." If she was going to stake out a career as a liar, she was going to have to start keeping track of the ones she'd already told. "Samoa. Right. No, not much ice. But I'm a dandy swimmer."

"I'll bet you are," he said appraisingly. "How about the hula? Do you do that?"

"That's Hawaii." Did he really think she'd fall for that easy a trap? Or maybe they really did dance the hula in Samoa. The next time she chose a birthplace, she vowed to make it somewhere she knew something about.

"So, are we going to rent skates? Or just watch?" she asked, purposely changing the subject as they neared the entrance to the ice. She took a closer look at some of the skaters. "I think we'd better stay here. They seem pretty good. I wouldn't want to knock anyone down."

There was one elderly couple skating out there, side-by-side, hand-in-hand, as melodic and smooth as if they were ballroom dancing. She had a long, pleated skirt with a little velvet jacket, and he had a short tweedy coat, worn with a rather dashing matching hat. Together, they twirled and glided over the ice, so perfectly in sync you knew they had to have been together forever, skating just like this.

"Wow. They really are good," she murmured, as the old man skated backward and swung his partner out in a practiced spin. "Did you see that? They weren't talking at all. He didn't have to tell her what he was going to do or anything, just nudge a little, and she knew exactly where to go. Wouldn't you love to be like that, so together that words aren't even necessary?"

Owen leaned in behind her. Softly, breathing into her ear, he said, "I thought you were the one who didn't think people should be together for longer than a month. I don't think you can learn to fox trot on ice in less than a month."

It was quite dark by now, even chillier, with the Christmas lights above the rink skittering in the wind, casting odd patterns of red and green on the ice. She could feel his presence there behind her, solid, hard, oozing heat. She held herself as still as she could, wanting badly to relax and go with the flow, but not quite able to, not when his words were skewering her.

"I didn't say people shouldn't be together," she corrected him, putting her arguments on automatic pilot. "I said *I* couldn't be together with anyone longer than a month. You keep making that mistake about me. I don't try to tell other people what to do. I simply share my experiences in the hope it helps other people understand their choices better."

"Right." His husky, honeyed tone told her he didn't agree, even as it made her tremble. Or maybe it was just the cold, knocking her knees and skittering up her spine, making her want to dissolve into his warmth. "If you say it's a mistake, then I'll have to try harder. I don't like making mistakes about you."

Her control was slipping, but she held on to the frayed ends as best she could. "How long do you think they've been together? Forty years? Fifty?"

"Long enough to know that independence isn't everything, I guess."

Stevie turned to face him. "Do you really think that? Do you really think that you, personally, would be willing to give up your independence for the right woman?"

"Absolutely."

"You say it so easily. But I don't think you believe it any more than I do." They were so close, and his eyes were so deep and his mouth so soft and delectable. She reached out her mitten, tracing his bottom lip, in the middle, at the fullest part, with her wooly thumb. She wanted to taste his kiss, but was she willing to bend that far to get it?

"I wish you could," he whispered.

"Maybe..." Maybe what? *Maybe I could give you a few nights to find out?*

But her thoughts were interrupted by the swooshing sound of a rapidly approaching skater. She turned, edging away from Owen and closer to the protective boards rimming the rink, as the same elderly lady she'd been watching earlier cruised up to the gate.

"You're very good," Stevie offered. "We've been enjoying your performance."

"Why, thank you, dear." She stayed where she was, beaming up at Stevie. "I saw you, too, and I just had to come over and tell you..."

"Yes?" *I recognize you and I've read the book? I saw you on TV and I think you're wonderful?*

"You really aren't dressed properly for this weather, dear. You're going to catch your death of cold." And then she skated away, back to her partner, content to have dropped her words of wisdom.

The skater's words were so unexpected Stevie burst out laughing. But the lady was right. Stevie wasn't dressed properly. She'd chosen style over substance, and now she was so cold through and through that her teeth were chattering, even as she guffawed with laughter. *This* was where pride got you.

As if in cosmic agreement with the skating lady's words, the clouds opened up and it began to snow softly, with big, fat flakes that drifted lazily to the ground.

As Stevie hooted, unable to hold it back to a polite level, she felt something cold and wet on the tip of her tongue, and she stretched it out to try to look at it. A snowflake! She made some mangled sound, something that was supposed to be, *Look, Owen, a snowflake on my tongue,* but came out more like, *Luh, uhen, anoway onnymun.*

Whether it was because she was making nonsense sounds, or because she had her tongue stuck out, or because she was practically jumping with excitement, she couldn't say. But Owen laughed, too, with a fresh, carefree sound that took her breath away. She put her tongue back in her mouth, and swallowed.

When he let loose, he sounded like...holidays. Like *It's a Wonderful Life.* Like total, unabashed joy.

She wanted that joy. She wanted *him.*

Her whole body was shaking now, and he pulled her closer, wrapping his muffler around her neck. Soft and warm from his skin, it smelled like him, too. Oh, God. Irresistible.

"You're freezing," he murmured.

She didn't care. "Owen, could you please...?" she began, but he cut her off.

He reeled her in with the scarf, he lowered his mouth to hers, and he kissed her, with all the heat and passion she knew they'd both been storing up since the moment they met.

His mouth felt slick and hot, his tongue plunging

into hers, starting a fire as surely as if he'd set a match to kindling. She heard herself release that same moan, the new sound that *he* stoked inside her, and hearing it seemed to inflame him all the more. Sliding his hands to her cheeks, he tilted his head so that he could delve deeper, branding her with his fierce, undeniable passion.

Stevie kissed him back with everything she had, unwilling to break the connection for even a second. If she could've climbed inside him at the moment, she probably would've jumped at the chance. As it was, she pressed into him, her calves, her knees, her thighs, trying to get closer to his blazing heat. She slipped her hands inside his soft camel coat, clutching at the wool of his sweater. Her extremities might've been icy, but she was melting from the middle out.

"Stevie," he whispered, breaking away.

"No, no." Greedy for more, she lifted her lips to his jawline, trailing kisses as she went. Her glasses had steamed over and she couldn't see much anymore, but that was more of a nuisance than anything else. She snatched them off with one hand, shoved them into his coat pocket, and went back to what she was doing. "Don't stop. Kiss me."

"Your skin is like ice. Your teeth are still chattering. We need to get you inside."

"I'm fine," she protested, winding her arms around his waist inside his coat. She didn't want to think about what might happen if they broke the spell of this moment, if either of them had a chance to think better of their crazy attraction. They had chemistry to burn, but they also had brains, and she knew what their brains would say. *Stop it, already!* That wasn't what she wanted to hear. "Please, let's stay here."

"We can't. I don't want your lips to turn blue or something." He dropped another kiss on those lips, lips she felt certain were not going to turn blue as long as he kept kissing them.

He backed up, drawing her with him. "Come on, Stevie. I'll take you home."

She was pretty much ready to do anything he wanted, although the idea of going home sounded depressing right about now. Home. To the Hotel Marceau. To Anna and questions and sanity, where kissing Owen was the worst idea in the world.

Damn.

But he kept stepping back, away from the rink, pulling her toward reality.

She made one last attempt, raising her mittened hands to his cheeks, lifting herself up high enough to press her mouth into his, to kiss him again, just in case it was her last chance.

"Come on, Stevie," he murmured. "Home."

Home. Well, her suite at the Hotel Marceau did have a fireplace. And maybe Anna wouldn't be there and they could turn the deadbolt and fasten the chain and toss off their clothes and...

That pleasant image was interrupted by a barrage of flash bulbs coming from about twenty feet away.

"What was that?"

"Someone taking pictures," Owen said curtly.

"Of us?"

"Who knows?" He kept Stevie pressed against his side, his arm firm around her. "Let's get out of here, okay?"

She smiled up at him, hoping against hope Anna wouldn't be in the suite when they got there. She wasn't quite ready for this day to be over yet.

8

"THIS ISN'T MY HOTEL," she said slowly, as they pulled up on a tree-lined street with houses on both sides.

"It's my place." After making that dramatic statement, he crossed around to her side, opened her door and extended a hand. "Come on."

"But I thought we were—"

"You thought wrong. Come on. The sooner we get inside, the sooner we warm you up."

That sounded kind of nice. He'd brought her to his house, and he wanted to warm her up. Men didn't say things like that unless they had plans. She couldn't say what those plans included, but she had hopes. Some brandy, maybe, or Irish coffee, tasted right from his mouth. Or drizzled on his bare skin. Yum. She licked her lips with anticipation.

She wasn't quite used to the idea that women like her did things like that, leaping from a few sweet kisses at the ice rink right to the bedroom—or better yet, the floor in front of the fireplace—but that's the way *he* thought she behaved all the time. Might as well enjoy her reputation. And earn it.

Looking around, she decided it seemed like a nice neighborhood, not fancy, but with people who cared enough to have shining Christmas trees visible inside the windows and strings of bright lights dangling here and there. It didn't look at all like the skyscrapers and bustling streets they'd just left in the Loop, but more like a neighborhood, and not at all where she would've imagined Owen living.

The house they were walking up to was two stories tall, square and boxy, made of some kind of soft gray stone. It was ablaze with lights on the first floor, including a candle in each window.

"You left candles in your windows?" she asked doubtfully, as he led the way up the steps to the front door.

"I have the second floor," he explained. He unlocked the front door, ushering her into an entryway. "It's a two-flat."

"Oh, okay." There was nothing wrong with the idea that he lived in the upper half of a house, but she was still confused. Except for his hand when he'd helped her out of the car, he hadn't even touched her. Her dreams of a cozy evening full of brandy and passion began to weaken. That was not the mood here. But she took the first step, looking back over her shoulder to see if he was following, hanging on to a few hopes that they could still make an intimate evening of it.

"Wait. We forgot the gifts." And then he left her there as he zipped right back out to the car to get the shopping bags they'd both overlooked.

Not quite the mad dash to passion she had envisioned. Stevie peeled off her mittens and earmuffs and sat down on the bottom step to wait for him. As she brooded over what was supposed to happen next, the door to the first floor apartment opened. A small girl in a red corduroy jumper peered out. "Who are you?"

I'm the cat your upstairs neighbor dragged home. "I'm

here with Owen. He lives upstairs. Do you know Owen?''

"Well, yeah," the child returned. "He's my uncle."

"Oh. Your *uncle*."

Owen had neglected to mention that he lived right upstairs from one of the four sisters and some undetermined number of the six nieces. Close family ties, indeed. Like, living-under-the-same-roof close. Like, hardly going to make noisy, passionate love right over his family's heads close.

"I'm glad to meet you," Stevie managed to come up with. "He told me about you."

Owen's niece just stood there, looking unimpressed. Maybe her uncle brought home strange women all the time. Stevie wished she could cross-examine this young miss about that very subject, but it probably would've been bad form, especially with him expected back any second.

Finally, the girl in the jumper twisted her mouth to one side and demanded, "Where's Uncle Owen?"

"He forgot something in the car, so he went to get it, and I'm waiting for him," Stevie explained patiently.

"Mooooooooom," the child wailed, leaving the door wide open as she ran back inside. "There's some lady here that Uncle Owen left on the stairs."

"What?" A taller version of the child, also wearing a red corduroy jumper, came to the door, with the little one peeking out behind her skirt. Both brunettes with pageboys and bangs, they were obviously mother and daughter. And the mom had a look of Owen about her, too, somewhere around the eyes and the cheekbones. Owen's sister fixed Stevie with the same suspicious look her daughter had tried about two minutes ago. "Are you waiting for Owen?"

"Yes, but he went back out to the car for a minute. We were shopping and we left the bags in the car, so he's bringing them in." Still carrying the earmuffs and mittens he'd given her, she smiled, rising, smoothing her skirt. "I don't know what's keeping him."

"I think you'd better come in. I'm sure he was going to bring you into my place, anyway. He doesn't keep much upstairs, in the way of hospitality," his sister confided, backing up into her half of the house. "I'm Lora, by the way. This is Hannah, my younger daughter. She's—"

"Seven?" Stevie guessed. "Owen told me all his nieces were between seven and eleven."

"She's eight." Lora's eyes, so like Owen's, were speculative and wary. Stevie could read the message behind them from here. *Funny, he didn't say anything about you.* "My other daughter, Courtney, is ten. She's getting some ribbon out of the craft closet. She'll be right back."

Stevie didn't know what to say. Craft closets? Mother-daughter jumpers? This was out of her range of experience. What had he been thinking, bringing her home to meet his family? His *family*.

The house was actually very nice, with high ceilings and dark wood floors, decorated mostly in white with primary colors here and there. The sofa where Stevie was told to sit was blue, the chair was red, and the painting behind the sofa was a block of bright yellow with a blue star smack-dab in the middle.

There was a Christmas tree in the corner of the living room, and oh my, what a tree it was, with long, sweeping branches and a major star on top. Every bough had an ornament or two, ranging from expensive blown glass to construction paper cut-outs of angels and gingerbread men. She could pick out cranberries and popcorn and pinecones, too, in lavishly draped garlands. The tree was going to collapse under all that weight if they weren't careful.

Although the house was otherwise neat as a pin, some serious work was taking place on the floor where Hannah crouched in the middle of a pile of fabric squares, felt scraps, scissors, yarn, glue and several different sorts of ribbon. Hannah was cutting a heart shape out of felt, very carefully snipping along with round-tipped scissors.

"Hannah, ask Ms...." Lora waited for Stevie to fill in her name.

"It's Stevie."

"Oh." Her tone went up an octave. "*Oh.* I see."

"Has he mentioned me?" she asked, surprised.

"He wrote a column about you." Lora's expression tightened. "I read all my brother's columns, of course."

"Of course," she said with a sinking heart, looking down at her "pseudo S&M wardrobe." What else had he said? Something about whips and spike heels and men begging for mercy. Oh, yeah. Destined to bring joy to the heart of his sister.

"Hannah, ask Stevie if she would like some cocoa or a cookie," Lora said politely.

Hannah rose reluctantly. "Would you like some cocoa and cookies?" she asked dutifully.

"Yes, please. Thank you." She clasped her hands in her lap, managing a smile, feeling like the worst sort of nuisance, and completely void of conversational charm. Where was Owen? How long did it take to haul in a couple of packages? And what was she supposed to say to his sister in the meantime?

"So he's interviewing you, is that it?" Lora inquired.

"Yes," Stevie responded, happy to have something, anything to talk about that did not include *What exactly are your designs upon my brother?* "He wanted to follow me around for a typical day, but he ended up convincing me to lead an untypical day. We went shopping and to an ice-skating rink. But we didn't skate. We just..." Kissed. "Watched," she finished up quickly. "Watched the other skaters."

"Uh-huh." Lora backed off, nearer the kitchen, taking Hannah with her. "Isn't that nice?"

"It was. Very nice."

His sister nodded. "We'll just... You know, the hot chocolate," she mumbled, disappearing around the corner, at the same moment another small brunette in a red jumper entered from the hall, and Owen came bustling in from outside. Finally.

He dropped his parcels and his coat near the chair, scooped up the second sister, who must be Courtney, and gave her a big hug. "I see you've met Stevie."

"Nope," Courtney said, disengaging herself and giggling as he tickled her. "I was getting ribbon." She held up a fistful of lacy package ties. "Mom and me were wrapping packages."

"Well, this is Stevie," he offered. He sent her a smile. "And Stevie, this is Courtney, one of my nieces."

"Yes, I met her sister a minute ago. And her mother."

"Good." Okay, so he was just clueless. So far he hadn't picked up on any of her I-want-to-kill-you-for-abandoning-me-here vibes.

He turned to Courtney. "Do you want to see what I got you for Christmas?"

She began to hop from foot to foot as she shouted, "Yes, yes!"

Lora returned, carrying a steaming red-and-white striped mug, garnished with a candy cane, which she set on a beaded coaster—also decorated to resemble a candy cane—near Stevie. Hannah brought up the rear, carefully balancing a small plate with exactly two cookies on it. They were sugar cookies, and they were shaped and decorated like, yes, candy canes. The mug matched the garnish matched the coaster matched the cookies, and the mother matched both daughters. Stevie began to sense a theme here.

Courtney was still hopping. "Uncle Owen, where's my present?"

"Owen, what are you doing?" Lora demanded. "You shouldn't be giving them their gifts now."

Stevie gratefully accepted the cocoa and let them fight it out.

"They should wait till Christmas morning," Owen's sister argued.

"You're no fun," he told her. All in one smooth move, he removed a small plate of cookies from Hannah's hand, placed it on the side table next to Stevie, and swept Hannah upside-down and spun her around a few times.

She began to squeal louder than Courtney had, as Stevie sank farther back into the couch cushions and tried to look inconspicuous.

"So," he said finally, dropping Hannah right-side-up, "everybody is all introduced, right?"

"Owen, you really shouldn't dump women on your

steps and leave them to fend for themselves," Lora chided. "Hannah found her and brought her in."

"Sorry," he said with a shrug. "But the good news is, the presents are here!"

Both girls immediately scrambled to the sofa to sit down like little ladies and accept their bounty. The fact that Stevie was already there gave them pause at first, but they worked it out, ending up with one perched on either side of her.

"I can move," she offered, half rising, but Owen gestured that she should sit back down.

"No, no, it's perfect this way, since you picked out the gifts," he announced.

"*She* picked out the gifts?" His sister's eyebrows rose all the way to her hairline.

Owen ignored her. "You're going to love what Stevie chose for you," he told the girls, opening the first bag.

"But Owen, we didn't wrap anything," Stevie protested. Looking at the fabric and ribbons on the floor, she got the idea this was definitely a wrapping home. Besides, she wasn't nearly as sure as he seemed to be that they would like their presents at all. She'd been thinking of little Britney Spears fans, not Suzie Homemaker girls in corduroy jumpers.

But he was already handing over the makeup kits. "Ooooh, wow!" Courtney cried. "Mom, look! Glitter makeup. I loooooove this!"

"Me, too," Hannah chimed in, dipping into a pot of blusher and propping up the mirror. Squinting into the mirror, she gooped a stripe of sparkly pink on her cheek.

Whew. They liked it. Stevie felt gratified by their

positive reaction, until she saw the look on their mother's face.

"Makeup?" Lora inquired in an odd voice. "*Glitter* makeup?"

But Owen was already offering them jewelry tattoos, which made the girls shriek with delight. Owen reached for another bag, pulling out a thick, sapphire blue sweater and a pair of jeans. Stevie didn't remember either of those items. He'd said he was going to buy something for his sister. Were these for Lora?

"Oh." He sat back. "This stuff is for Stevie."

"You bought that for me?" Wow. When? She searched his face for clues. "Between ladies' lingerie and the Frango mint counter? But..." Hesitating, she attempted to phrase this carefully. "Please tell me you didn't purchase the other, um, item we discussed."

If he pulled big, fat cotton underpants out of his bag of goodies, right here in front of his sister, and then explained why he'd felt it was necessary to offer them to Stevie, she would be forced to kill him.

"No, I left those behind," he said, his eyes sparkling with amusement. "You seemed pretty sure you didn't want those."

Phew.

He leaned across the coffee table, proffering the clothes he'd bought her. Damned if they didn't look awfully tempting. But then, so did he.

Stevie smiled, extending both hands, accepting his gift. Funny how different a sweater and jeans could seem after a few hours outside in the cold. He stayed where he was, tilted across the coffee table, his eyes holding her. "Thank you," she mouthed. "I love them."

"I thought the blue would look nice with your

eyes." He winked at her, and her stomach did a cart-wheel.

"With my eyes. Oh." The fake blue eyes he was so entranced with. Looks like she'd be keeping the contacts for a while.

"Hey, where are your glasses?"

She blinked, touching her face, expecting them to be there. When had she lost her glasses? Oh, yeah. When he'd kissed her and the steam rose so high between them that she couldn't see anymore. "They're in your coat pocket," she said awkwardly. "I stuck them there when... When we were at the skating rink."

He winked at her again, damn him. As he went to retrieve her glasses, Hannah demanded, "Where's the rest, Uncle Owen? *Our* stuff. You said there was more."

Pretending to grumble, he dropped the wayward glasses in Stevie's lap, and then went back to the shopping bags, flipping clothes out right and left, making his nieces giggle as he made missiles out of their gifts. He dished out leopard print separates in Hannah's size, and zebra in Courtney's, shoving things around until he found all the various bits and pieces, earning himself several hugs and kisses by the time everything had been distributed.

The girls were running around putting on their backpacks and trying on their boots until Lora interceded.

"Okay, okay, enough," she declared. "Daddy will be home soon, so let's pick up everything, thank Uncle Owen and his friend Stevie, and then put it away, okay? Then I want you to come back here and show Stevie how to make ornaments for the tree, while Mommy and Uncle Owen have a chat in the kitchen."

As Hannah and Courtney dutifully scampered off, their arms full of jungle print clothes and accessories, Lora took her brother's arm and pulled him back into the kitchen. "We'll just be a second, Stevie. We have some, uh, family business to discuss. Who's got who in the Christmas exchange, you know."

"Sure." Stevie fingered the soft sweater in her lap. He'd bought blue to go with her eyes. Was that the sweetest thing she'd ever heard or what? A girl could get really attached to a guy like that.

She wondered if she could ask for somewhere to change into the new clothes. It hadn't been that long ago she'd thought these bulky things were insulting. Now she wanted to shed her Stevie Bliss leather and slip right into the sweater and jeans.

The girls weren't back yet, so she rose from the sofa with the clothes, intending to just pop into the kitchen, ask Lora where she could change, and then pop out again. But she heard low, intense tones, and she didn't want to intrude, so she stood there a moment, waiting for a pause in their conversation.

"How could you?" Lora's voice demanded, rising enough that Stevie could hear every word. "Owen, you brought someone like that into my home, near my children? What were you thinking?"

Stevie closed her eyes. She hadn't harbored any illusions that Lora liked her, but she hadn't realized it was this bad.

"I didn't bring her in. Hannah did," he returned coldly.

"Did you see her idea of suitable gifts?" she hissed. "It's like she wants to turn my children into junior versions of *her*. Junior hookers!"

His sister had just called her a hooker. Stevie put a hand over her mouth. She felt like throwing up.

"Lora, that is totally unfair," Owen said angrily. "Don't you dare say another word about Stevie. She did me a favor. She was kind enough to help me pick out things the girls would like. And they did. It looks to me like she knows more about normal kids than overprotective mothers."

"I know why you bought her those clothes, Owen," she announced in a superior tone. "It's pretty obvious you were embarrassed by the way she dresses. And why not? She dresses like a slut. Well, *my* brother is way too good to be wasted on a slut."

Owen's voice dropped into a more persuasive register. "Listen, Lo, don't worry. She isn't the way she dresses. I know she has a hard exterior, but that's not who she is inside."

This just kept getting worse and worse. It wasn't bad enough that his sister hated her. She could get over that. But he agreed with her. Owen, her hero. He agreed with his snotty, holier-than-thou sister!

"Besides," he went on, "I think I can change her."

She felt like screaming. Scum, scum, scum. He was scum. She bit down on half her hand to keep quiet. He thought he could change her? Her? When her persona was carefully crafted to reflect market surveys out the wazoo? And he wanted to change her?

"Oh, Ownie, you can't change someone. You know that," Lora told him, sounding aggravated but loving all at once. Stevie could image her thumping her little brother on the head as she spoke. Very Judge Hardy.

"It's more like getting her to see who she really is and less like actually changing her into someone else."

"You're such a do-gooder," his sister said with affection. "Always trying to fix the wounded birds."

Okay, that was enough. Eavesdropping on conversations where she was bad-mouthed was one thing, but she absolutely would not stand there and listen to Owen and his sanctimonious sister call her a wounded bird. She wanted out of this cozy house with its handmade ornaments and its candy cane coasters. She wanted out!

So she backed up into the living room, cleared her throat loudly, and then clomped her heels against the hardwood floor as she retraced her steps back to the kitchen. "Sorry to interrupt," she said with saccharine charm, "but I really need to get back. Hooky can't last forever, can it?"

"Stevie, if you'd like to stay for dinner..." Lora began.

"Oh, no, I couldn't." *And foist my hooker self onto your family? Yeah, right.* "You've been so kind, Lora. Thank you."

"Are you sure?" Owen asked, quickly joining her. His eyes searched her face, and she wanted to say, *Don't worry, I'm pretending I didn't hear any of what you said to your sister, you scumbucket, you.*

"This has been fun, but I think we're done now," Stevie said cheerfully, taking a step away from him, putting some distance between them. She couldn't very well give him back any of the things he'd already given her, so she shoved the sweater and jeans and even the earmuffs under her arm. "Could you take me home please? Or should I call a cab?"

"I'll, uh, drive you back to the hotel," he mumbled.

"Good." And that was the last word she spoke to

him until his car pulled up in front of the Hotel Marceau.

"Stevie," he said finally, breaking the silence. "Is there something wrong?"

"I'm just tired." She practically leapt out of his car. "See ya."

As far as she was concerned, that was the last time she would ever see Owen Dasher.

9

Bliss Hits the Spot
By Owen Dasher, *Chronicle* Columnist

Call me a convert.

I happened to take in another stop on the Stevie Blitzes Chicago Tour the other day. Not a bookstore this time. Nope. Our girl went back to high school for some one-on-one with the senior class at the Brody Academy.

I know what you're thinking. Stevie Bliss, influencing the innocent minds of high school girls? Isn't that, like, totally whacked?

Not as whacked as you might think. Turns out Stevie Bliss has a point. Heck, she has several.

She told the young ladies at the Brody Academy the absolute truth. Men don't always treat women as well as they should. It's fair and it's smart for women to be picky, to do what they want and not to sell themselves short for the sake of a relationship.

I agree with Stevie Bliss. All the way.

Readers of this column know that I have a mother, four sisters and six nieces. I've told you before that I sometimes find them baffling and disturbing, that I often lament the gap between the sexes.

But I also respect my mother, my sisters and my nieces. I hope they respect themselves, too.

And when I listened to Stevie talk turkey to a bunch of high school girls, when I heard how they responded, I realized how important her message is, not just to the senior class at Brody Academy, but to a whole generation.

I hope my nieces will grow up and listen to voices just like Stevie Bliss.

ANNA WAS HUMMING some stupid carol along with the radio as she put another bulb on the tiny Christmas tree she'd set up in their suite.

"Could you please turn that off?" Stevie snapped. "I'm trying to concentrate."

"What are you so cranky about? He practically nominated you for sainthood in the last column."

"Hmph." If she were being honest, she didn't know what to make of that column. He was a convert? Not hardly.

Yet it wasn't like Owen to be so completely dishonest. What game was he playing, anyway?

So she ignored that irritatingly cheery column and did the research she should've done before she ever met him. She pulled open her laptop, searching the archives of the *Chicago Chronicle* for every old Owen Dasher column she could get her hands on.

"Mr. Social Reformer," she muttered, paging through another one. "Mr. Champion of Lost Causes. Mr. White Knight riding in on a charger to show people the error of their ways. Yeah, that fits."

"What are you mumbling about now?"

"Nothing. It's just..." She turned to Anna. "When I

met him, I thought I was playing *Basic Instinct.* And instead, it's *Pretty Woman.* And I hate that movie!"

"Stevie, you know very well that makes no sense to me whatsoever," Anna shot back.

"*Basic Instinct,* no underwear, dangerous woman, hot sex, drives guy crazy," she explained in shorthand. "*Pretty Woman,* hooker, reformed by gifts and love from a good man. Yuck! And I'm not a hooker, either!"

Anna planted her hands on her hips and glowered at Stevie. "I don't think I even know who you are anymore."

"You're still mad because I got out from under your thumb for a few hours." Stevie pushed away from the laptop. "Well, get over it."

"Stop blaming everything on me," Anna said acidly. "We both agreed to this scheme in the first place. We both bet our futures on it. Remember?"

"I suppose."

"And you aren't even trying anymore." Anna shook her head. "You run off with some guy. You diss a radio station and leave me to pick up the pieces. And now you're yelling at me, when I'm sorry, but I'm totally blameless. Just because you couldn't keep your hands off the reporter is no reason to take it out on me. I'm not the one who ran around Chicago and made out with—"

"Couldn't keep my hands off? Made out with?" Stevie repeated. "What do you mean? Who told you that? I never said—"

Anna cut her off with a wave of her hand. "You haven't told me anything about what happened that day. But it's in the paper. Don't even bother to deny it. There are pictures."

"Pictures?" she shrieked. "Pictures?"

"Read it and weep." Anna sifted through a pile of clippings. "I got it yesterday, and I didn't say anything because it's not like it's bad publicity. But if you're getting all googly over him and it isn't going well, that's still no reason to blame me—"

Stevie snatched the article from her friend's hand. It appeared to be a gossip column, and not from the *Chronicle*, but one of their rival papers. Sure enough, there was a picture of the two of them, apparently taken at the skating rink. It showed Owen lassoing her with his scarf, and her nuzzling him, gazing up at him like an adoring fool, as if he'd just invented penicillin and found a solution for world peace, all in one big snowball of fabulousness. It was hideous.

"Dasher & the Vixen," she read out loud, unable to believe her eyes. "The well-known *Chronicle* reporter and a certain sexy single spokeslady were caught canoodling all over town last night. Will Stevie Bliss toss out the Single 4-Ever mantra if Dasher has the reins? Or is she taking him for a fast ride to Dumpsville on Santa's sleigh? Stay tuned. Our sources tell us the heat between these two is enough to melt the North Pole."

She blinked, letting the paper dangle from her hand.

"So," Anna said briskly, "does Dasher have the reins? Were you really canoodling in public?"

"I never heard the word canoodling before." She swallowed. "If it means what I think it means, I guess we were. I mean, not very much. Just a few kisses. Not hot sex or anything. I mean, for the minute there, I was hoping... Never mind. We did not melt any Poles." She took a deep breath, trying to brave it out. "But so what if our canoodling made the paper? Isn't that good for my rep? One more guy I've bagged? I mean, we've planted stories like this before. Without the pictures, of course."

"Maybe. But the others were planned." Anna chewed her lip. "I'll be honest, Stevie. This one scares me. I'm worried about him. Like maybe you're falling for him for real."

"Don't give it another thought," she said hastily. "I'm not falling anywhere! So I lost my head for a few hours because I was stressed out from the book tour. You and me, we haven't sat still for one minute since this thing kicked off. And I guess I needed a few hours away from it, away from being, you know, Stevie Bliss, media creation. But that's it. A few hours. I had my mental health break. It won't happen again." She tried to appear contrite. "Promise."

Anna perched on the arm of the sofa, setting an arm around her friend's shoulder. "Stevie, sweetie, we're pals. You can tell me, right?"

"Tell you what?" she asked warily, not sure she wanted to follow where this was going.

"If you need to schedule time to get away, you tell me. Because we can do that," Anna assured her.

Stevie stifled a sigh of relief.

"I mean," Anna went on, "yes, it's the Christmas season and every day counts, but we can find an hour or so here or there to get you away from the glare. If that's what you need, I mean, for your mental health."

"No, I'm fine," she managed. Not quite a raving lunatic just yet. "Fine."

Anna leaned back farther on the couch, frowning as she pondered. "Sex could be a wonderful stress-buster, you know. Did you ever think about going

ahead and boinking his lights out, just to get it out of
your system?"

Stevie jumped up so fast, she almost knocked Anna
over backward. "Not a good idea."

"Okay, well, I guess that answers that."

"What's that supposed to mean?" she demanded,
spinning around to face her friend.

"That if you're that defensive about it, you've obviously thought about it," Anna answered logically.
"And why not? I've seen the chemistry myself. You
have to have considered it."

She couldn't hold it back one more minute. Considered it? She was practically obsessed with it. Even as
mad as she was after the hooker remarks in his sister's
kitchen, she still *wanted* him. She wanted him bad. The
Stevie Bliss they'd concocted would've taken him
without a backward glance. She would've yanked
him inside the other night, ripped his clothes off, satisfied her lust, and then thrown him out on his White
Knight backside.

But Stephanie... Stephanie couldn't quite pull it off.

"So?" Anna prompted. "Have you considered it or
not?"

"It's all I think about!" she confessed. In the old
days, she'd shared every thought with Anna. But she
had been keeping her feelings about Owen Dasher to
herself. She hadn't said anything about him or their
playday, not the kiss or the baby, not even the elf. And
certainly not the underwear. She shuddered.

"Well? What?"

"Anna, things did not go well. But I can't get him
out of my head. I want him."

"Then why don't you take him?"

"Can't." She tossed herself back onto the sofa, lifting both hands to bracket her head. "I mean, I would love to. I would love to *scorch* him, you know. Boink him so hot and so bad that all he can do after is lie there and whimper. But..."

"But?" Anna demanded. "Well?"

She sank down farther into the cushions. Where did she begin? There were so many reasons... "For one thing, he thinks I'm so experienced, that I've been with so many men in so many ways. What would he do if he found out I don't know anything?" she argued, her voice rising as she got into her subject. "And it would be pretty obvious, don't you think? I mean, *me*, scorching him with my wicked boinking ways? I don't have any wicked boinking ways!"

"Oh, yeah. Point taken." Anna sighed. "I guess you really shouldn't risk it. Not with a reporter. He can say you're a tramp all he wants in the paper, but if he says you're bad in bed, the whole thing is over."

It was deflating.

Her co-conspirator in all things Stevie Bliss slid onto the couch next to her. She seemed to mull the situation over for a few seconds, and then she continued in a no-nonsense tone, "Okay, well, no harm, no foul. I mean, his last column was fine. I prefer controversy, but I'll take a valentine. The other reports are great, too. People are talking about you, and that's exactly what we want. If you don't want to sleep with him, I respect that."

"I do want to. I just can't!" she persisted.

Anna narrowed her eyes. "I don't care what you do as long as you don't get into some gooey, head-over-heels, serious thing with everyone speculating about what's going on and turning *our* media circus into a totally different media circus."

"Gooey? Head-over-heels?" Stevie echoed. "Moi?"

"You're human," Anna said grimly. "I can see you, without thinking, falling into some kind of...relationship. Like, see you tomorrow. And tomorrow. And tomorrow..."

"Not with him," she returned tersely. "Not with him."

Anna shook her head again. "I'm still worried about you. I see you going all mushy on me and we can't have that. He talked you into playing hooky, didn't he? Who knows what else he can talk you into?"

"I've explained that," she protested. "I told you, I just needed—"

"I know what you said. I'm not sure I believe you." Anna patted her knee. "Listen, Stevie, you can have relationships later. After we sell another million books. But for now, we need you sassy and single. And that means without Owen Dasher. Okay?"

She didn't answer. She was thinking that maybe Anna wouldn't worry so much if she knew the rest of it, about the disapproving sister and the kitchen morality play. There was no way she could've started any kind of relationship with him, even if she had wanted to. His sister thought she was a slut. "And in his heart, so does he," she whispered. *Can't sleep with him because I'm not enough of a slut, can't keep him because I'm too much of a slut.* It made her head hurt.

But Anna had moved on. Standing, she paced back and forth, and Stevie knew her well enough to know she was planning ahead, the way she always did. Anna found comfort in laying out plans. "We're in the middle of our tour," she said briskly. "We have a stop in Indianapolis next week and Minneapolis and St.

Louis the next. So let's focus. Let's get back on message, okay?"

"Have we not been on message?" Stevie asked dryly.

Anna sent her a caustic look. "If all anyone is talking about is whether you're falling in love with this guy, they lose sight of the book completely. They think Stevie Bliss is just as vulnerable as anyone else and that all our talk about independence and self-reliance means nothing. Is that what you want?"

"I'm not in love with him and I'm not falling into anything!" Stevie said again, louder this time. "He doesn't even like me."

"Which is why he wrote this column about what a peach you are, right?"

"Oh, he may say in the column that he sees my point, but it's not true. Not really." She sent her friend a bitter smile. "In his heart, he thinks I'm a fallen woman or something, and I need to be lifted. The *Pretty Woman* thing. Remember when you looked at his old columns? I read them today. Full of reclamation projects. That's what he sees in me. One more fixer-upper."

"Don't sell yourself short."

"I'm not. I'm being perfectly honest," she contended. "He doesn't respect me the way I am, and he thinks he can change me. He said it right out loud. How could I want any man who only wants to change me?"

Anna's eyes reflected concern and something else—pity maybe—as she hovered there, in front of the fireplace. "Be careful, okay? Guys with Galahad complexes can be very seductive. And very dangerous."

"I'm fine," she responded wearily.

"Before you know it, you're in love and you're trying desperately to be whatever it is he wants you to be." Her friend grimaced. "And then when you don't change—because no one can, not really—he dumps you. Pain. Heartache. Totally not blissful. It's *wrong*."

"I don't think he would—"

"Just stay away from him, okay? If he calls me, I'll tell him your schedule is full. If he manages to get through to you, you promise me you will tell him the same thing," Anna said sternly. "You promise."

"I promise."

"Good." Anna leaned over and patted her arm. "Okay, now you need to call the radio station you blew off and apologize. I tried to set up a new interview and they were pretty annoyed. I think you'd better try to make amends. We're burning one press bridge, and we're going to need as many others as we can build."

"All right already." Closing up her laptop, closing her mental book on Owen, Stevie took Anna's cell phone and dialed the number she was given. "Hi. Is this Wendy? Wendy, this is Stevie Bliss. I was supposed to be on your show—"

But the woman on the other end cut her off. "Stevie, I'm so glad to hear from you!" she exclaimed.

"Well, good. I wanted to apologize—"

"No apology necessary. Listen, Stevie, can I tape you? I would love a quote to play on the air."

"Sure, I suppose. Why not?"

"Great. One quick quote." In the background, Stevie could hear the click and whir of a tape recorder switching on. "My listeners are dying to know, Stevie. Has Dasher tamed the Vixen?"

"What?"

"Has Dasher tamed the Vixen?" the announcer repeated.

Dasher? And the Vixen? This goon wanted to know if Owen had tamed *her*? As in, bent her to his will, molded her like clay, turned her into Susie Homemaker just like his insufferable sister? "No!" she shouted. "Never."

And she hung up the phone with a clatter.

"HAS HE CALLED?" Anna asked, biting her fingernail.

Stevie concentrated on her lip liner. She squinted into the mirror, making the line perfect. "I haven't talked to him. I haven't seen him."

"I didn't ask that." A long pause hung between them. "So he *has* called?"

"Maybe," Stevie hedged. She'd only hung up on him thirteen or fourteen times in the last three days. "I don't know."

Anna seemed to be satisfied with that answer. They were both on edge. Too many days answering too many people who wanted to know what was up with "Dasher and the Vixen." Whoever thought that little catchphrase up ought to be killed, as far as Stevie was concerned.

"Are you ready for this thing tonight? There's going to be press crawling all over the Field Museum for this charity bash," Anna told her. "You need to be on your game." She peered into the mirror over Stevie's shoulder. "You look a little tired."

"I'm fine. Makeup is a wonderful thing," Stevie said brightly. "So, who do you have lined up as my date, anyway? I hope it's someone really dishy. We need to have my picture taken with him and splashed all over the place to stop all this nonsense about..."

Ooops. Her mouth was running away with her. "Never mind."

"He's a baseball player," Anna rushed to tell her. "From the White Sox. A pitcher, I think. He has a real reputation as a ladies' man, and he should be just the ticket."

White Sox. Was that the team Owen's mother liked? Or the other one? It really didn't matter, did it?

"Sounds good." She filled in her lips with blazing red color, one of the newest shades in the Glam line. Good old Glam. It seemed like so long ago she and Anna had thought that with some Tae Bo and a few Glam products, they could rule the world. Little did they know...

"I think this will really spike your rep as a bad girl," her friend said eagerly. "I've also leaked a few rumors that he's Mr. December, to, you know, get people off this, uh, Dasher thing."

"Excellent."

"Okay, so..." Anna backed up to the doorway. "I'll just reconfirm the arrangements with his people. Be right back."

Stevie stuck her index finger into her mouth and plucked it out again with a smacking noise to make sure she didn't get lipstick on her teeth. Man, she really had the makeup routine down, didn't she? Stevie Bliss, Glam Queen.

She rose from the vanity, moving to check on the outfit she was wearing for a photo shoot later that afternoon. She was just slipping the loose black silk blouse off the hanger when Anna came back, her eyes wide, her square jaw clenched.

"What is it?" Stevie asked. "The baseball player can't make it?"

"No, no, he's all set." Anna hesitated, sort of dithering with her hands, which was something she never did.

"Well? What?"

"I went over the guest list, the whole guest list, I mean, so there wouldn't be any surprises." She let her voice trail off. "And... Guess who else is on the list?"

Stevie's heart seemed to stop for a second. She already knew the answer. "Dasher."

"Yup." Anna moved closer, her hands positively shaking by now. "Is that okay? You still want to go?"

Yes! But then again... *No.*

"Why don't you come with me?" she proposed, trying to put a brave face on it. "You can watch out for me, make sure he doesn't bother me. That's a good idea, isn't it, Anna? You never get to go to these fancy dress things. It could be fun."

"I can't," Anna stammered. "I don't have anything to wear, and besides, I, uh, have to go to Indianapolis."

Stevie was confused. Anna seemed really hyped about this, which was very strange. *She* was supposed to be the basket case, not Anna. But then, Anna had been getting weirder and weirder every day. "I thought Indianapolis was tomorrow?"

"I was going to go tonight instead. To set up early," she said quickly.

Hmm... Something was going on here. Something weird, and it had to do with Anna. Had Stevie been so wrapped up in her own bad mood that she'd completely missed the signals?

She tried to adopt one of Anna's firm, take-no-prisoners attitudes. With a level gaze and a severe look, she announced, "I think you'd better tell me what this is about."

"Well, if you must know..." Anna raised her chin. "I have a date."

Stevie felt her eyebrows go through the roof. "Tonight? In Indianapolis?"

"He has something to do with the Pacers," she said in a rush. "I met him a few days ago. The day you played hooky. I was trying to track you down and somehow I ran into him and he was so nice... As long as we were going there tomorrow, he asked if I could come a night early and go to a game with him. I know it sounds like I'm jumping ship, but it's just this once, and we were going to Indianapolis, anyway, and you had the charity thing, and I thought it might be okay—"

"Whoa! Calm down. Slow down." Her head whirling, Stevie took a seat on the edge of the bed. No matter what else happened, she knew in her heart that Anna was way overdue for a night out. The poor thing had practically taken a vow of chastity when she'd signed on as Stevie's assistant. So if the new excitement on Anna's social calendar was surprising, well, it would have to be accommodated, wouldn't it?

"Listen," Stevie said suddenly. "This is no problem. I'll be fine at the charity bash. So what if Dasher's there, too? Think about it. He'll undoubtedly have a date. I'll have a date. What better way to show people we're not together than for both of us to be at the same function with other people?"

"If you *stay* with other people," Anna said doubtfully. "You know how he gets to you. Are you sure you can handle this?"

Stevie pasted on a wide smile. She owed this much

to the friend who had given so much over the years and taken so little. Anna deserved a carefree evening in Indianapolis, secure in the knowledge that Stevie could take care of her own lousy agenda for once.

"No problem," she declared. "My baseball player and I will be a big hit. You'll see us in tomorrow's papers."

10

OWEN NURSED HIS DRINK, staring over the balcony down into the main hall of the Field Museum where the big dinosaurs were lined up. He saw the huge, arching bones of a real dinosaur, the amazing Sue the Tyrannosaurus Rex, as well as a few grande dames of Chicago society who were equally skeletal and fit the description of "dinosaur" equally well. He hated shindigs like this, where the usual upper-crusty suspects came out to swill champagne and hopefully hand over big buck donations for a good cause. But the *Chronicle* was one of the sponsors of this particular event, and he had been told to make an appearance, tuxedo and all.

It wasn't the place that bothered him. He actually liked the vast Field Museum, with its exotic artifacts and amazing collections, and he'd brought his nieces there more than once to see the Egyptian tomb and the man-eating African lion display. That one was Courtney's favorite because it was scary, whereas Hannah preferred to ooh and ah over the baubles in the new exhibit on pearls.

But he didn't have the kids with him tonight, and it was a whole lot less fun. He glanced at his watch, wondering how long he needed to stay to fulfill the obligation. Maybe if he had another drink, strolled around the soaring columns on the main floor, shook a few hands, made small talk with some bigwigs...

But when he looked up, his eyes caught a splash of scarlet against the wide white expanse of the grand staircase.

Stevie.

She was at the other end of the hall, one floor below him, but even at that distance, even from behind, he knew it was her. It was the way she held herself, the way her hips swayed as she moved up the stairs, the way her startling red dress, cut straight down to the floor and slit up to a place that was nobody's business, seemed to rip a hole in the stuffy atmosphere of the charity benefit. One spectacular leg emerged from the bold slit as she took a step up, revealing her from red stiletto heel all the way up to her thigh, and he choked where he stood.

Even if she'd had a tarp over her head, he'd have recognized that impossibly long, shapely leg anywhere. Displaying it like that, she might as well have punched him in the gut.

What was she doing here? And who was she with? She had her arm linked through some joker's, a tall, athletic type with his head turned away as they paused there on the stairs. "The rock star?" Owen ground out. "Or some new Mr. December?"

Sloshing his drink in his haste, Owen pushed away from the gallery railing. He had to get to the stairs. Now. He had to see her. He had to find out who she was with and... He had to do *something*.

By the time he'd managed to thread through the crowd milling around on the balcony, making his way all the way around and down the grand staircase, Stevie and her escort had disappeared from the stairs.

He hadn't passed her, so his best guess was that she'd gone back down, into the main area of the party. Owen descended the rest of the way into Stanley Field Hall, where buffet tables and cocktail rounds had been set up under the eye of the museum's immaculately preserved elephants. He hailed a passing waiter and nabbed a fresh drink, gulping it in one swallow and handing back the empty glass.

Brooding, feeling unfamiliar jealousy fester inside him, he stalked down one side of the hall and up the other, winding around the gleaming white columns that lined the immense, skylighted space, getting farther and farther afield. This was maddening. Had she ducked inside an exhibit, still clinging to that creepy date? Where the hell was she?

And then he heard her laugh. That was Stevie all right, with the husky, intimate giggle that sounded as if she'd just shared a very private joke. His hands knotted into fists. Laughing? She was here with some other guy and she was laughing like *that?*

He followed the sound, finally locating her directly above him, not far from where he'd been when he first spotted her. Stuffing his hands in his pants pockets, Owen backed up and craned his neck. She and her escort seemed to be holding court, standing very close together, smiling and talking to an animated cluster of people. Oh, man. He recognized the guy. That was no rock star. That was a baseball player.

"Joe Verdana. The pitcher," he said with surprise and disgust. Verdana was notorious for picking up groupies on the road, sometimes two and three at a time. No class, no morals, just a ninety-five-mile-an-hour fastball and a penchant for beaning batters who crowded the plate. What was she doing with him?

His temperature continued to rise as he watched the two of them. He generally didn't spy on people from across crowded rooms, but he was willing to make an exception. He was outraged. Stevie, out in public, draped all over a creep like Joe Verdana when she wouldn't even take *his* calls.

"Yeah, that's probably how most stalkers feel." A stalker. That's what he had become. He retreated farther across the wide hall, trying to get a better angle. "I don't get it. We had a good time. Everything was going great. So what is her problem?" he muttered.

"Hey, Dash, watch it."

He wheeled, holding out a hand to steady the man he'd almost knocked into. It was a photographer from his own paper. "Sorry, Mac. You're covering the benefit, huh?"

"Yeah. The place is crawling with photogs." Mac jerked his thumb up toward the balcony. "So what's up there that you're trying so hard to see?"

"Nothing. Nobody."

"Uh-huh. So you wanna look through my zoom at whatever it is you don't really want to see?"

Oh, bad idea. But he did it, anyway, holding the camera up to his eye, adjusting the zoom lens until he could see every eyelash. He clenched his jaw. She had her hand on Verdana's arm. She was smiling up into Verdana's smug face. And the pitcher's beefy arm was draped around her, giving her a squeeze every now and again. A more than friendly squeeze. So much for her high-minded ideals about being picky and holding out for the right man. Joe Verdana was no one's idea of the right man, not even for a month. Not even for one night.

"Who *is* she?" he asked.

"You don't know who she is?" Mac took back his camera and looked for himself. "Isn't she the one you've been writing about?"

"Yeah. I thought I knew her, but this isn't who I thought she was. I guess I don't really know anything about her," he concluded. "Except that she's slept with most of the male population of the northern United States. Except me."

"Well, if it's any consolation, I haven't slept with her, either," the laconic photographer commented. He frowned, peering through his lens. "Looks like that guy has, though. Or maybe later, huh?"

Owen shook his head, trying to keep himself from bounding back upstairs and knocking Joe Verdana over the balcony. With his luck, the pitcher would land right on Sue the dinosaur and crush the heap of million-year-old bones. He could destroy a prehistoric treasure and a major league pitcher in one fell swoop.

"Stevie's not worth it," he said under his breath.

Why did he want her so badly? He took one look at her in that damn red dress, and he was dying to drag her out of there and make love to her, up against the nearest wall if that was the quickest way to get rid of this insanity. Up against a wall? That wasn't like him. There was no way he was going to give in and connect purely on a sexual level like every other man she knew.

And how many of them were there, anyway?

Part of his problem was just how frustrating, irritating and wounding to his stupid male ego it was to think about where she'd been and who she'd been with. And how damn many men had been there before him.

He narrowed his gaze, keeping her in view as he

cooled his heels down there in the main hall. She seemed to be sticking close to Verdana, damn her hide, but he knew he could catch her sooner or later.

He ambled up the stairs, waiting for his chance, cutting through one knot of party-goers and then another, edging closer. He knew the precise moment she saw him, too. Her eyes widened, her cheeks flushed with a shade more color, and her fingers went white around the stem of her glass.

God, she looked gorgeous. Her hair was styled more smoothly tonight, and it shined with golden streaks under the twinkling party lights. She had come out without her glasses, and as usual, seemed to be suffering no vision problems without them. But the blue of her eyes was so clear and bright, he felt like he needed sunglasses just to blunt the effect.

And the dress... That dress should've been illegal. If he'd harbored any illusions that Stevie wore undergarments, this night and that dress would've clued him in. There was simply no way you could put anything under the paper thin fabric—sliding over her skin like a fall of water—without giving it away.

He knew it. She knew it. Everyone at the party knew it.

She was naked except for a few yards of scarlet silk.

And that knowledge only increased the physical pain he was feeling, as he tried desperately to keep himself in check. As he looked across the balcony at her in that dress, his teeth ached. His palms began to sweat. His whole body hovered on red alert.

He tipped his head to one side, judging just how far up the slit in her dress went, letting his eyes touch what his fingers couldn't, telegraphing his thoughts to her, wanting her to know and feel his scrutiny. Her gaze flickered away and she offered a thin smile, pretending to have heard whatever joke it was the others were laughing at. But she sneaked a peek back in his direction, and he felt victorious.

Still here, Stevie. Waiting.

Finally, after Owen had stood there for long minutes, doing nothing but stare at her, several of the people in her group inched away. And then a few more. Until it was just her and her baseball player, both looking bored.

"Verdana!" someone cried from behind Owen. "Hey, buddy, you want to come over here and sign something for this lady? Big fan, buddy. Big fan!"

"Sure, sure," the pitcher called back, immediately striding toward his new audience. Leaving Stevie completely alone.

Her mouth opened and closed, as her eyes seemed glued to Owen's face.

His cue. He smiled as he circled around behind her, getting the three-sixty on the dress and the slit and her high, tight little bottom, molded perfectly by the thin silk.

"Go away," she said flatly. "My date will be right back."

"If he does, you can tell him his month is up a little early," he murmured, leaning in close.

Looking straight ahead, not at him, she took a quick swallow of wine. "I only met him tonight. His month hasn't started yet."

"So maybe he's on an accelerated schedule." He was breathing in her ear when he said, with a fair amount of intensity, "Tell him if he lays a hand on you, I will make sure he never pitches with that hand again."

She gulped. "You've got to be kidding," she said, sounding flustered. "As if caveman tactics would impress me."

"Did you read my last column?" he asked darkly. "I tried the nice guy approach. I actually said I agreed with you. That got nowhere. So I'm changing my style."

"It's not working." She tried to brush past him, but he caught her by the hand.

"Tell me, Stevie. I'm curious. Why haven't you considered giving me a month?"

"Give you a month and you'll take a year," she scoffed, holding herself at arm's length. "I know you, Dasher."

"Is there something wrong with that?"

"It's not my style."

"So give me the month," he countered, using her own arm to tug her closer. He closed his eyes as he bent nearer, his cheek next to hers, breathing into her ear. "Move in with me, make love with me. See what happens."

He could feel her shiver next to him. So faintly he could barely hear it, she whispered, "That's exactly what I'm afraid of."

"Stevie..."

Once again, she tried to break away, and he held on to her hand. Carrying herself with dignity, her pointy little chin in the air, she said, "Tell me. That last column, where you agreed with me, did you believe what you said? Did you really think I had a point? I mean, is it a good thing for a woman like me to stay single?"

"A woman like you?" He had to be truthful. It was the curse of the ethical man. And he truly didn't believe Stevie was meant to be alone. She was meant to be with him, picking out tiger-striped booties for their babies. Oh, God. Where did that come from?

"Well?" she asked again. "Tell me the truth, Owen."

"The truth? No. I don't believe you'd be better off single."

"Then why did you write that?"

"I don't have to believe it," he tried. He was so tired of this. "I know *you* do. That's good enough. Because..." He released a long breath. "Because I want you."

She looked down at her hand, clasped so tightly inside his. Her gaze lifted and met his, but she left her hand where it was. He could still feel her trembling, her resolve weakening, and he needed to make love to her so badly at that moment that he couldn't see straight.

"Stevie," he said again, in a rough, rasping voice he didn't even recognize. "Don't walk away. Stay with me."

"Shhh. Don't say anything, okay? Just..." She licked her lip, backing away, drawing him with her as she retreated hastily into the shadowy corridor of one of the exhibits. "Owen, I want you to kiss me."

He certainly didn't have to be asked twice. Right there in some crazy little booth, partially hidden behind red velvet curtains, he snagged her around the waist, pulling her and that scandalous dress hard up against him, claiming her mouth with one hungry, fierce, possessive kiss, unwilling to wait even a second longer to taste her. Her hands tangled around his neck and she shoved her fingers into his hair, pushing up into him, making incoherent little noises that drove him insane.

She stumbled back, taking him with her, right into the control panel that ran the exhibit. Pressing backward, she hit a button right under her bottom, and then jumped back to her feet as they were surrounded by twinkling stars. Hundreds of them.

It was bizarre, to so suddenly be bombarded with stars. Incredibly romantic, but bizarre.

He couldn't help it. She felt so good, and that dress... He slipped one hand up inside the high slit in her skirt, sliding over soft, smooth, bare skin, rounding the curve of her bottom, molding her to him. He couldn't breathe, couldn't think. But if he didn't start thinking soon, if he didn't slow this down, he'd be slamming her up against the glass under all those stars, taking her right here, right now.

Panting, he pulled back, holding her steady with one hand, reluctantly removing the other from under her skirt and patting the fabric back into place. "Stevie, you are—"

But she cut him off, sticking two fingers over his lips. She was breathing heavily, her breasts rising and falling provocatively under the thin silk of her dress, and her lips already looked bruised and well-kissed. "Do not say that I am something else. Good, bad, whatever. I don't want to go there again."

"You are incredible," he finished. He brushed his lips over her fingers, moving them aside, lowering his mouth to hers again, but softer and slower now, sliding his tongue ever so gently into her wet, warm mouth, enjoying the way she whimpered when he did.

"Ahem."

He figured it out first. Caught. Red-handed, so to speak.

Owen yanked her behind him, shielding her completely, as he straightened and turned to face a grinning brunette in a black dinner suit.

"Hi," she said gaily. She walked closer, yanking the curtains all the way back. He'd seen her before, but he had no idea who she was. "I'm Wendy Weiss. Wendy in the Morning? On KJ03?"

"And?" he demanded

"Oh, no," Stevie groaned behind him.

"So, Stevie, that is you back there, isn't it?" Wendy in the Morning tipped her head to one side. "And you still say there's nothing going on between you two?"

"No comment," Owen said between gritted teeth.

"Oh, wait. That wasn't what I asked, was it, Stevie?" Wendy began to laugh, and it echoed off the glass behind them. "I asked if it was true that Dasher had tamed the Vixen. But judging from the way you guys were going at it, nobody has tamed anybody here."

"I'm sure you'll excuse us." With Stevie's hand securely in his, he edged out of the booth, searching for the most direct path to the exit, not looking back.

All he wanted was for the two of them to be out of that museum, in his car and back to a place with a bed. Within five minutes, if possible.

STEVIE STILL couldn't quite believe this was happening. She punched the code into the elevator so fast she hurt her hand, but Owen kissed it for her, so it wasn't like she cared. The heat between them was threatening to knock her off her feet, and the sooner they got to her suite, the better.

But she was clumsy with the key, and he finally took it away from her, crashing open the door, wrapping her in his arms and kissing her all the way in.

She flipped the light switch on and he turned it right back off again. "Anna?" he whispered into her mouth, not loosening his grip one iota.

"Out of town," she breathed back.

"Good." He tossed her coat aside. "Why is there a fire already in the fireplace?"

"Gas. Bellboy turns it on every night."

"Good."

She shoved his jacket off his shoulders and backed up, pulling him farther inside. She tried to reach down to take off her shoes, but he growled, "Leave them on."

Oh. Liked the strappy red stilettos, did he?

She smiled. Playing with Owen was lots of fun. She turned away, but he reeled her back in. She reached for the buttons on his shirt, but he held her hands. After a moment, he stripped off his own bow tie and undid his collar, popping a few shirt studs as he went.

Then he said, "That dress," in a raspy undertone that slithered down her spine.

With a wicked smile, he shoved his hand into the slit, harsh and ferocious, ripping the fragile fabric up to her waist. The noise seemed to echo in the quiet room, shocking them both.

"Sorry," he whispered.

It felt breezy down there. And very erotic, especially with his strong, long fingers still clasped on her hip. Tingling, edgy, unsteady, Stevie tried to remember to breathe as she traced a finger along the line of his jaw. "It's okay. I wasn't really planning on wearing it again."

Good. I don't want you ever wearing anything like that again."

He brushed his thumb up near her belly button and she sucked in air, dizzy, on fire, itching to move, dying to be touched. His hand teased her stomach and then danced lazily back to the torn edge of the silk, testing the threads, barely grazing her skin. No kisses, no other touch, just that slight, delicate sensation of the tip of his finger high on her thigh. She held her breath, afraid to move, afraid she would betray the secret, that she was already wet and ready, from the inside out. Did he know? How could he not?

Finally, he lowered his head, nipping at her mouth, tantalizing her with brief, tempting, unsatisfying kisses. But every time she tried to take it deeper, he pulled back.

"Owen, don't make me wait," she threatened. She was twitching with impatience, her hands fisted on his chest, by the time he finally slid his fingers around to the round curve of her bottom, nudging her closer, trapping her up against him.

"Ohhhhh," she shuddered, dragging her hands behind his head, lifting herself into him.

He felt wonderful. *She* felt like a starving woman, more than ready to start the banquet.

Every inch of him pressed into her, hot and hard, head to toe, and she wanted him with everything she had and everything she was. "I don't think I can wait," she murmured, swaying slightly in his arms, rubbing up against him with her cheek against his, the rock-hard evidence of his desire pressing into her stomach, and her breasts, slippery in the silk dress, creating exquisite friction against his chest. "Now, okay? Here. Now."

"Standing up?" He laughed. "Fine with me. I've been ready to go off all night, you know. You standing there naked in that dress." He took a deep, shaky breath. "There are some wonderful things about hooking up with a bad girl."

Stevie went still. "A-a bad girl?"

Why couldn't she stop thinking? She wanted to give in and make wild, mindless love, nothing to do with good or bad, naughty or nice, just Owen and Stevie and a whole lot of skin. *Owen. Inside me. It can be if I let it happen. Don't think until morning. Just do it.*

But... But she pushed away. It wasn't that easy to turn off her brain.

"Is that what you want?" she asked slowly, trying to read the expression in his eyes in the dark room, lit only by the glow of the fireplace behind them.

"You know what I want," he said greedily, corralling her again and trying to kiss her.

But she held herself as far away as she could within the iron circle of his arms. Frustrated, upset, she shot back, "I know you want me. But is it because you think I'm a slut? Are you looking for a hot, nasty ride on the Stevie Bliss express? Is that it?"

It was his turn to go still. "Is that what you think?"

"Yes," she whispered.

A long pause hung between them. Owen took a step backward, dropping his hands from her.

"What is it?" he asked finally. "What's wrong with me? Why can't I have a month like everyone else? You've had so many men. What's one more?"

Each word lashed her like a whip. A month like everyone else... Had so many men...

Holding her dress together, trying to keep herself covered, Stevie lifted her chin, refusing to be cowed.

"Do you think this is a competition?" she cried, aching for him to tell her she was wrong. "So that's it? You want your month with me, just like everyone else?"

"Why not?" he demanded.

Smashing her hand through her hair, she stumbled backward. "I don't even have a movie for this. This is beyond *Pretty Woman.* Beyond *Basic Instinct.* Beyond *The Postman Always Rings Twice.* And it sure as hell isn't *It's a Wonderful Life.* We've moved into new territory,"

"What are you talking about?"

"Did you ever think that maybe I don't want you for a month? Maybe I don't even want you for tonight," she cried.

Owen's expression was arrogant and cruel. "We both know that's a lie," he snapped.

Humiliated, she realized he was right. Her body no longer had any secrets from him. It had already betrayed her when it flamed everywhere he kissed her and trembled everywhere he touched. Like Pavlov's dog, it reacted exactly the way he expected. She practically sat up and begged.

She thought she might throw up.

"I-I have to leave," she mumbled, pushing past him, scrambling to find her coat.

"Stevie, this is your suite. *I'll* leave."

And without another word, he cut a wide path around her, grabbed his jacket and slammed out the door.

She stood there for a long moment, still not exactly sure what went wrong, except she was pretty clear it was her fault, whatever it was.

One other thing was clear. She would be going to bed alone tonight.

Alone. Blissfully single. Wasn't that how it was supposed to be?

11

SOMEHOW SHE MANAGED to wrangle the whole phone over into the bed. Propping herself up far enough to be able to talk into the receiver, she dialed the hotel in Indianapolis.

As soon as she heard a voice on the other end, she launched into her prepared speech. "Anna? Sweetie, I'm sorry but I'm, uh, not feeling well. I don't think I can make it to Indy this morning, so I'm hoping it won't be too awful for you to cancel everything for me there. All right? Not too impossible?"

Anna didn't say anything for about fifteen seconds. "Was he there last night?"

"Yes," she said tightly.

"And you saw him?"

"Yes."

"And you slept with him?"

"Not exactly."

This time the delay was more like a whole minute. "I'll be right home."

AS NOON ROLLED AROUND, Stevie was sitting in the breakfast nook, wearing her favorite pink poodle pajamas, tucking into her third doughnut. If the truth were told, she was already full.

"I bribed the concierge twenty bucks to find me a

box of Krispy Kremes," she muttered. "I'm not stopping until I eat every one or die in the attempt."

That would make a great headline. Bliss Blows Up After Mad Doughnut Binge.

She was saved from that unpleasant fate when she heard Anna's key in the door. Tossing half a doughnut back in the box, she didn't bother to rise, waiting at the table until Anna rolled her suitcase around the corner.

Anna raised an eyebrow. "You look like hell. I've only got one thing to say..."

"I told you so?" Stevie asked in a sing-song voice. "Or maybe, sheesh, Stevie, I leave you with one instruction—stay away from that guy!—and what do you do? You screw it up!"

"Neither." Anna slung her coat over her suitcase and dropped herself into a chair opposite Stevie. "What I have to tell you is that the book and the Stevie Bliss persona aren't worth this much misery. I think you should go find him ASAP and tell him the truth." She waved a hand up and down at Stevie. "Show him who you really are, poodle pajamas and all."

"I can't."

"Yes, you can," Anna argued, propping her elbows on the table and leaning in. "We didn't start this so you could be miserable. It was supposed to be about choices, not about shutting a door on something before it even begins."

"But, Anna," she wailed, going back over all the territory she had already considered and reconsidered all night long. "That would be like turning my back on everything that *Blissfully Single* stands for. I believed in it when we put it together and I still believe in it."

Anna rolled her eyes toward the ceiling. Displaying very little patience, she declared, "So don't marry the guy. Just sleep with him. Have fun with him. See what it can be. Maybe it won't last a month. Who knows? Who knows till you find out?"

Stevie had thought she couldn't feel any lower. She'd thought wrong. "Oh, God, you sound like *him*. That's what he said."

Anna yawned. Pushing herself away from the table, she moved to the sofa instead, where she sat down and kicked off her shoes. "I'm sorry, Stevie, I really am. I don't know what to tell you. I had to catch a plane and rush right back here and I am very tired. So you'll have to excuse me if I'm not picking up on the subtleties of your non-relationship with Owen. If you want him, go for it. *Try.* If you don't, don't."

"So I guess your date in Indy went pretty well, huh?" Stevie inquired. "For you to come home and totally change your tune like this."

"It was okay. I'm not running off and marrying this guy, if that's what you think." Lying back into the couch, Anna pillowed her arms under her head. "But I did decide that there might be life outside our book tour."

"This is so not like you," Stevie said, stunned.

"Oh, come on. We knew it would come sooner or later. We even talked about it, about what might happen if one or both of us, you know, fell in love. For me, who cares? So the faithful assistant has a boyfriend. So what? But for the poster girl..." She seemed to be looking for patterns in the ceiling tiles. "It's problematic."

"I think we're focusing on the wrong thing here.

I'm not in love," she protested. "I'm not thinking of leaving the *Blissfully Single* movement. Not at all."

"Oh, yes, you are. Don't kid a kidder, babe." Anna sighed. "I don't know what happened last night between you and Sir Galahad, but here's my take on it. He came on strong, you melted into a puddle, you scared yourself, and you made up something stupid to push him away." Adopting a babyish voice, Anna said mockingly, "'He doesn't love me. He doesn't respect me. He writes all kinds of nice things about me in the paper but he doesn't mean it.'" She cocked an eyebrow. "Am I close?"

"Not really," Stevie lied. Was she really that transparent?

"Yeah, whatever. I know you, Stevie. I know you're nuts about this guy and he seems nuts about you, too. So he's conflicted and he's making mistakes. You think you're not?"

Well, that was certainly a telling point. Making mistakes? How about jumping his bones under a canopy of primeval stars with a reporter right around the corner? *I want you to kiss me, Owen.* Yeah, right.

Could Anna be right about the rest? Could she really have brought up the whole good girl/bad girl thing just to give herself a convenient excuse to run away from him?

Oh, jeez. She hated it when her own emotions were so complicated. And cheesy.

"Sooner or later, you're going to have to admit you want to see what there is with this guy," Anna said matter-of-factly. "For you, I admit, the timing is definitely lousy. I mean, deciding you don't want to be the carefree single girl anymore in the middle of the Christmas season kind of sucks as far as book promotion goes." She shrugged, lifting her shoulders off the couch. "But maybe he's worth it."

When Stevie didn't respond, Anna sat all the way up. "Stevie?" she ventured. "Is he worth giving up *Blissfully Single* for?"

"I don't know."

"I know one thing." Heaving herself off the sofa, Anna trundled over to her suitcase and started to roll it back to her room. "Stevie, you need to do something. You're a mess, babe."

Where's the Bliss?
By Owen Dasher, *Chronicle* Columnist

Okay, so I was had. I'm a guy. We're easily confused.

Remember how I told you Stevie Bliss had a point and we should all pay attention and...zzzzz...

Sorry. I'm boring even myself.

Anyway, I was wrong. No point. No meaning. No nothing. That's the sum total of Stevie Bliss. She's a fraud, folks.

Oh, yeah, she's sporting a pretty nifty package, emphasis on package. As in, prepackaged. As in, all marketing and no meat. As in, all sizzle and no steak. It's worse yet when you get right to the center of Ms. Bliss, where you find... Zero.

She pretends to be this hot hootchie mama, yet it seems clear she would fold like a three-day-old newspaper if the Right Guy gave her a wink. Sure, she's been through more men than Ball Park has franks, and none of them tempted her to stay on the straight and narrow. But don't kid yourself. They were all lightweights and losers.

If Stevie Bliss met up with someone who could really challenge her, give her as good as she's giving out, you gotta know she'd change her ways so fast she wouldn't know what whipped her.

I know there's been a lot of speculation about what's going on between yours truly and Ms. Bliss. Well, nothing's going on. You heard it here first. But I can guarantee that if it were, the lady would not be protesting. She wouldn't be cutting out after a month, either.

I may not be the Right Guy, but I bet you a nickel she wouldn't be throwing me out like cheap Christmas trash.

OWEN PUT the finishing touches on his column, gave it a last once-over, and pressed Send. He was late and he needed to get it out of there, so he might as well be done with it and put it in someone else's hands.

Besides, it said what he wanted to say. And whether he liked it or not, it said what people wanted to hear. He and Stevie were some kind of "It" couple, even if they weren't a couple. But his numbers were going through the roof, and everybody wanted more column inches from him, especially if they concerned *her*. He had become a phenom. They were talking about running his column every day. All because of *her*.

"Hey, T.J.," he barked across the newsroom. "What have you been doing?"

"Huh?" She meandered over, taking her time. "About what?"

Surly and impatient, he drummed his fingers on his desk. "I asked you to dig up stuff on Stevie Bliss at least two weeks ago. What did you find? Come on. It can't take that long."

"Sorry," she told him. "I've been trying. Whoever she is, or whoever she was, she didn't leave much of a trail. I came up empty with Samoa and the Peace Corps. I'm still trying to check on married couple anthropologists. There are more of them than you'd think." She paused. "I don't suppose you have fingerprints or DNA or something actually useful?"

"Why would I have fingerprints or DNA?" he asked, baffled.

"Well, I don't know." T.J. lifted her narrow shoulders in a shrug. "She didn't, you know, leave any on your, um, clothes or anything?"

On his clothes? "What are you talking about?"

"The online edition of *Inside Chicago* has pictures of the two of you making out under some goofy star thing," she said reasonably. "Didn't you see it? The headline is kind of funny. Dasher Blitzes Vixen. What with the starry backdrop and your head on her neck and her head kind of, you know, arched back like a porn star, it was hard to see the details. But I figured if you were up that close and personal you might have, oh, I don't know. Bodily fluids? Hair fibers?"

She was waiting for a response, but he was so taken aback, he didn't have one. Sucker punched. He felt sucker punched. When he finally spoke, it came out strangled and choked, something simple like, "Oh, no."

"Poor Owen," T.J. said sweetly. She looked as if she were trying hard not to come right out and snort with laughter. "Does the tic in your jaw mean you're having problems with your vixen?"

"She's not my vixen. She's not a vixen at all," he tried, not even thinking about what he was saying.

"So what is she?"

"I don't know. Oh, man," he groaned, dropping his head to his hands. "I don't know. That's the problem."

"Better figure it out. You're the guy with all the answers, right?"

"ANNA? ANNA?" Stevie stormed. She slapped the newspaper down on the table. "Did you see this? Did you see? Now he says I'm a piece of meat!"

"Actually," Anna returned dryly, "he said you were all marketing and no meat."

"I don't care. This is awful. Much worse than pseudo S&M with whips," she muttered, pacing back and forth in front of the breakfast nook, retrieving the newspaper so she could wave it like a banner. "I mean, at least that was vaguely sexy. But all marketing, no meat? All sizzle, no steak? A big zero? He says I'm a big zero!"

"Obviously, he did not appreciate whatever stunt it was you pulled the night I was in Indy."

"Why are you so calm about this?" Stevie demanded. "I think you should be calling our lawyers. I think I've been defamed."

Anna didn't even look up, just continued to proofread the press release she was preparing. "Give it a rest, Stevie."

"I haven't even gotten to the worst part yet. I mean, setting aside the crack about how I've had more men than Ball Park has franks." She wondered if steam was really coming out her ears or it just felt that way. "Did you see this, Anna?" Brandishing the paper, she looked for the exact wording. "He says I would fold like a three-day-old newspaper if the Right Guy gave me a wink. He says I would change my ways so fast I wouldn't know what whipped me. Whips again! I think he has a fetish."

"You must bring out the whips in him," Anna said pleasantly.

"And what is it with him and this Right Guy business? He says that twice, about the Right Guy. And he capitalized the *R* and the *G*." She pointed to the relevant lines. "What does it mean? Can you answer me that?"

"No, Stevie, I can't answer that," Anna said automatically. Edging around in her seat enough to fix Stevie with a glare, she picked up her volume. "Except that, *duh!* Earth to Stevie. Obviously he thinks *he's* the right guy or he wouldn't be capitalizing it."

"Him? The right guy? There's no such thing!" Stevie trumpeted. She'd been waiting for her opening. "That's proved by the fact that Owen wants me, someone he knows is a made-up, faked-out version of a human being. How can he be the right man if there is no right woman? Because there isn't. He came right out and said I'm a fraud. And he's right. I am totally a fraud. *Now,* I mean. I didn't used to be. So who was I then, when I wasn't a fraud?" When Anna didn't provide an answer, she leapt forward with one of her own. "I'll tell you who I was. Stephanie Blanton. Remember her? He would never have looked twice at Stephanie Blanton. Never. Which proves he is *not* the right man."

"Wow, I'm impressed." Anna went back to her press release. "You really thought this all out, didn't you? You sound all logical and everything."

"Are you making fun of me in the hope I will calm down and comes to my senses?"

"Yes," Anna said politely. "Is it working?"

"No."

But Stevie shut her mouth, deciding it was useless to try to convince Anna of anything. She stomped off, heading back to her bedroom.

"Where are you going?"

She mumbled, "I have to look for lingerie."

"Lingerie? Since when do you own lingerie?" Her interest piqued, Anna followed Stevie. She paused in the doorway, watching as Stevie plowed through her drawers. "Okay, Stevie. I have one for you. Did you ever think maybe he's smitten with the real Stevie, you know, the one inside? Not Stephanie. Not Stevie. But where the twain meets?"

"Not for a minute."

"You certainly took your time with that answer," Anna offered in a mocking tone.

Stevie heaved a huge sigh. She made it a good one on purpose. And then she sat on the edge of her bed, clutching an old T-shirt and a pair of panty hose, staring into space.

"I am going to be painfully honest with you, Anna. Owen is the best man I ever met." She swallowed, trying not to get too sentimental. "He's funny and smart and principled, even kind of sweet." She remembered their hooky day and the expression on his face when he gave her the blue sweater. "Very sweet," she said softly. The blue sweater. To match her blue eyes. And that just proved the point, didn't it?

"So what's the problem?"

"I don't have blue eyes." She shook that off. "He is the best man I ever met, and yet he's still as shallow as the rest of his species," she announced angrily, slapping clothes out of her drawers so fast they were a blur of colors. "It has nothing to do with the person inside. He gets turned on by a pair of blue eyes, some front-and-center cleavage, and a come-hither look. And I can prove it."

Slowly, Anna asked, "What did you have in mind?"

She came up with the small bag she'd been looking for, the one from Marshall Field's lingerie department. Waggling it in the air, she declared, "I am going to prove to you, to Owen, and to myself, that this is all about sex, all about the fantasy person you and I invented, and that there is nothing real here at all. Not one real thing."

"You're not thinking about doing something stupid, are you?" Anna came closer. "Because you know you don't have to prove anything to me. I believe you, one way or the other. No rash, meaningless gestures necessary."

Stevie's answer was to pull out the cream-colored chemise, the one with the red ribbons and the tag that said Open Me First. "He set down a challenge in that column of his," she insisted. "And I'm going to answer. We'll see who gets whipped."

"Stevie, this has gone too far. Let it go. He can't hurt you. It's just another column. It's good publicity," Anna tried.

"Forget publicity." Stevie set her jaw. "This isn't about publicity. This is personal."

12

OWEN WAS SITTING at his desk with his head in his hands, brooding. He did a lot of that these days. He heard the commotion begin somewhere near the elevator, and he lifted his head, curious. There were hushed voices, a scramble of feet and chairs and some real momentum going on there. Whatever it was was headed his way.

He saw her the second she rounded the corner. Stevie. And yet not Stevie. Some new, even more torturous version.

Her hair was a mess, all wild and free, and she hadn't bothered with the glasses. From her chin to her knees, she was covered in red fur. Fake fur, anyway. It was as if she'd mugged a bright red Yeti and stolen his coat. She was clutching the fuzzy monstrosity closed in the front, and he was very afraid there would be nothing underneath it. She was definitely headed for him. What for?

Was she going to shoot him? Stomp on him? Drown him in red fur?

His mouth went dry as she advanced on him. Except for the coat, all she appeared to be wearing were red, high-heeled leather boots.

Red fur, red boots. She might as well have broadcast to the nation that she was a Scarlet Woman.

The entire newsroom seemed to hold its breath, as

people scattered, giving her room, shooting rapt glances back and forth between the two of them, as if it were some ridiculous tennis match.

"Should I call security?" the reporter at the next desk asked anxiously, reaching for his phone.

"No." Owen half rose, leaning on his desk. He met her gaze. "What do you want, Stevie? What are you doing here?"

But she didn't say a word. Her mouth, a slash of red lipstick, twisted into a sneer.

"What do you want?" he asked again.

She snapped, "You. Now."

"And?"

"No and. That's it." She reached over his desk, grabbed him by the tie, and yanked, hard. "Come out from behind there. You can run but you can't hide."

"You don't want to do this. You're making a spectacle of both of us," he tried to argue.

He couldn't help but notice that her coat had drifted apart a few inches when she went for the tie, revealing a good deal of creamy skin but also some kind of abbreviated white garment underneath. He let out a sigh of relief. At least she wasn't naked. At least she didn't seem to be planning to strip right there in the newsroom and get them both arrested or something.

"*I'm* making a spectacle? Yeah, like you haven't already done that in your column?" She laughed, but it was taunting and humorless. She gave his tie another jerk. "Come on, big boy. Show me what you've got. Show me exactly who's all marketing and no meat."

A collective "ooooh" sound filled the newsroom, indicating that everyone there thought she'd scored a direct hit with her last comment.

"Hey, Dasher, I think you better give the lady what she wants," somebody said with a guffaw.

Sure, they all thought it was hilarious. But how long would it be before somebody less juvenile walked in here and took a less humorous view? Owen glared at them, hoping to quell more jokes before they got started.

"Stevie," he said more softly, trying to reason with her. Although she still had a firm grip on his tie, he edged out around his desk. "Why don't we get out of here, make this more private, so we can talk?"

"Talking wasn't exactly what I had in mind." But she spun on one dangerous red heel, her hair and coat flying, and beat a quick path back to the bank of elevators. "Come on, Dasher. I haven't got all day."

Once again, the crowd parted like the Red Sea to give both of them plenty of room.

She stabbed the up button, which seemed strange. There was nothing on the higher floors of the *Chronicle* Building he could imagine she would be interested in. Surely she didn't want to take their fight to the roof?

Or maybe she did. Maybe that was the idea. To toss him off into the hard, cold streets of Chicago.

When an elevator arrived and the doors opened, Christmas music poured out. The tinkling sound of "Rudolph the Red-Nosed Reindeer" was not exactly the right mood for this occasion, but Stevie marched in without a backward glance. She wheeled back around to face him, holding the door, waiting. "Get in," she ordered.

He didn't deal well with orders, but going with her was better than staying in the newsroom after what his colleagues had just witnessed. He got in.

As soon as the doors closed, he turned to her, looking for some trace of the woman he thought he knew. "I take it you didn't like my column. Is that what this is about?"

She shrugged. "Did you expect me to like it? It was insulting and rude and..." As if she sensed she was losing her self-control, she bit off her sentence. "You push me. I push back."

"What are you trying to do, Stevie?" he whispered. "This is crazy."

"We're going to do things my way," she said coldly, waiting till they'd cleared the fourth floor and then the fifth before she pulled a key out of her pocket and inserted it in the panel.

"Where did you get that key?"

"I got lucky." He could tell she was struggling to turn it, forcing the key all the way to the left. "Your maintenance woman is a fan of my book."

The elevator thumped to a halt, jolting them both. A red light that said Out of Service began to glow. Stevie carefully removed the key and jammed it into her boot, tapping that foot until the key clinked down all the way.

Between floors. Out of service. Trapped. With Stevie Bliss looking very much like a woman with a mission. Vengeance? Payback? What kind? Oh, God.

"Stevie..." he began, but she smiled and it was so chilly and heartless it scared him into silence.

She dropped the coat, kicking it behind her. She stood before him, wearing nothing but those damn boots and a slinky little slip with red ribbons on it. It covered practically nothing. Its off-white color didn't hide the rosy circles of her nipples, peeking through the bodice, or even the shadow at the apex of her thighs. She might as well have been naked. But seeing her charms through the filter of that filmy, transparent fabric made it worse, somehow.

His mouth began to water.

The slip was sinfully short, cut low in the front and barely making it past her derriere in the back. It seemed to be held up by the ribbons, one white one and one red. The red one skimmed one shoulder and down the front, intersecting with another red ribbon under a bow and a tag that said Open Me First. Oh. He got it. She was supposed to look like a package wrapped just for him.

Somewhere along the line, between the time she'd shucked the coat and now, when she just stood there, roasting him with her eyes, the Open Me First tag lifting and falling every time she took a breath, his heart seemed to have stopped.

"You wanted sex. You wanted your chance to prove you were better than all the rest," she breathed, advancing on him. She shoved him up against the wall of the elevator with all her might. "You got it."

"SANTA CLAUS IS COMING TO TOWN."

The music was all wrong. If she could've removed a boot and smashed the speaker with the heel, she would've. But she didn't see a speaker. And she had to play her Bad Girl scene to the sound of "Santa Claus is Coming to Town."

So far, she was pushing forward her agenda based solely on adrenaline and fury. But if he kept looking at her like that, if she had to listen to one more silly Christmas carol, she didn't know how long she could keep up the act.

Yes, when she smashed him into the wall, there was definite heat in his gaze. Smoldering, dangerous heat.

But there was heart there, too, as if he was afraid to touch her for fear of where they might go, of how hurt they might be when it was done.

She didn't want him to feel or think. She just wanted hard, nasty sex, hot and incredible, everything he imagined from the bad girl he thought she was, to sear his brain and his hide with her imprint so that he would never forget who he'd tangled with.

Stevie Bliss, Avenging Sex Goddess.

But inside... Inside she was pleading with him to see through the act and turn this idiotic scheme around.

She could see his pulse jumping and she knew he was holding himself back with a supreme effort of will. Damn him. He wanted her. They both knew that. And the unmistakeable bulge in his pants pretty much gave the game away, anyway.

She grabbed handfuls of his shirt and ripped it open, popping buttons, exposing his bare, beautiful chest, leaving only his stupid tie dangling there. Although he slipped the tie off, he didn't say anything, didn't make a move toward her.

She ran her hands over the muscled expanse of his chest, flicking his nipples with her nails, trying to inflame him. When that didn't work, she pressed her mouth up into his, kissing him for all she was worth. And he didn't respond.

She swore something ugly under her breath, stalking away, pacing back and forth, kicking the coat. "What are you waiting for?" she jeered. "I'm here, I'm ready, I'm the tramp of your dreams. What are you waiting for?"

"Maybe I don't want you that way."

"We both know that's a lie," she said, echoing his

words from the other night, staring rudely at his crotch. "What's the matter, Owen? Don't think you can handle me?"

A low growl escaped him. He bridged the gap between them with two long strides. This time *he* shoved *her* into the wall, catching both her hands in one of his, holding them above her head, bending her body into his.

The position made her breasts fuller, higher, and they threatened to spill out the front of the skimpy chemise. Her nostrils flared as she tried to get air into her lungs, oxygen to her brain. This was what she wanted, wasn't it? Mindless, out-of-control passion?

Trying to provoke him, she raised her knee, rubbing it against the outside of his pants leg, locking the bottom halves of their bodies together.

Her chemise was too short, too skimpy, and it had ridden up enough to leave her bare below the waist. Owen wasted no time sliding his free hand under there, urging her up and in, so that her tender flesh fitted precisely against the hard ridge of his erection. "Ohh," she cried. "Ohhhh."

And then, as his mouth covered hers and he swallowed her moans, he kissed her deep and hot, rocking her there, back and forth, wedged between his hard body and the wall. Oh, it was fabulous. She could already feel herself throbbing, climbing, flooding with desire.

She wanted to touch him, too, but the more she struggled, trying to free her hands from his grip above her head, the tighter he held her.

Pulling back, away from the kiss, he breathed heavily, staring down at her for a long moment. She felt pinned by his gaze, trapped by his fierce grasp, and she wiggled against him, which only made things worse. Sparks seemed to shoot through her body, and she whimpered with need as the sheer silk of her bodice brushed his bare chest, teasing her nipples. Her pelvis ground into his, trying to find the right place, the right rhythm, to fill this huge hunger.

Slowly, deliberately, he hooked a finger under the thin red ribbon at her shoulder, barely touching her at first, then jerking it harder so that the slick fabric of her bodice edged up and down, chafing her erect nipple. He bent his head, licking her through the silk, sucking her taut peak into his mouth, biting down gently, using his tongue and his teeth and the wet silk against her.

He slipped his free hand down between them, touching her at her most vulnerable spot, where she was already coming apart at the seams. He slipped one and then two fingers inside, and she couldn't stop the shudders wracking her, the mounting pressure. With his mouth on her breast and his fingers stroking her, pushing her, she was so full of sensation she had nowhere to go but up, into him, crazy and dizzy and desperate, dissolving into a shattering climax.

He staggered back, dropping her hands, and she almost fell to the floor without the pressure of his body holding her fast. It was a rude re-entry to the real world, where Santa Claus was still coming to town.

"He's not the only one," she whispered in a shaky voice.

Owen held out a hand. "I delivered," he said cruelly. "How about the key?"

"But Owen, I'm not done with you yet." She smiled, knocking him gently, so that he fell backward onto the fur coat. She was already climbing on top of him, reaching for his belt, unzipping his pants and yanking them out of the way.

If he was fighting at first, he stopped that pretty quick. Under her, around her, he arched up and into her, and she found herself crying out again with the sheer power of this erotic bliss.

But then he flipped her over, so that he could set the speed, and he slowed things way down. It was maddening. He kissed her, he held her and he stroked inside her again and again, stoking the fire between them into newer, even more incredible flames.

How was it possible to feel so much? How was it possible to want him so much?

She ran her fingers over his muscled chest, filling her hands with him, still greedy for more. The fur coat was soft at her back, and Owen was slick and smooth against her skin, and she relaxed into the warmth of these new, heady pleasures.

Yes, the heat between them was amazing. Yes, she felt desire leaping in her veins. But she felt more.

Oh, no. She felt more. Her heart swelled as she hugged him tight, finding his mouth, trying to tell him with sweet, soft kisses that she'd been wrong, that it wasn't all about sex, that there were deep, deep feelings here, too.

But the passion climbed again, and her mind was too full of it and him to think clearly. He whispered her name in a throaty whisper, spending himself within her, and she tumbled head over heels into another climax, holding on to his sweat-slicked skin for dear life.

Content in this strange afterglow, she fastened her arms around his neck, listening to his heartbeat. Her new emotions spilled out before she could stop them. She whispered, "What if I think I love you, Owen?"

He raised himself up on one elbow, flashing her a smug, satisfied smile. What did that mean? As he bent to nuzzle her shoulder, his grin widened.

Well? Was he going to say anything in response to her declaration? Or leave it hanging there?

"Stevie, Stevie," he said softly, dropping kisses along the slope of her neck, "I hate to say I told you so, but I did."

That wasn't what she wanted to hear. "What do you mean?"

"I knew I was the right man to tame you," he claimed, looking quite pleased with himself.

And why wouldn't he? She'd probably been the easiest lay of his life, screaming like a banshee and coming more than... More than Santa Claus in the damn song.

"Admit it, Stevie," he went on. "That was the best sex you ever had, and you aren't going anywhere for a good, long time. 'Cause you already admitted it— you love me."

She leapt up, ripped the chemise off her body and threw it at him. As he stumbled to his feet, she wrapped herself in the fur and then sat down abruptly, trying to get her boot off to get to the key for the elevator.

With one boot on and the key in hand, she warned, "You'd better put your pants on."

With the key back in the slot, she turned their love nest back into a functioning elevator, slapping the button for the next available floor, refusing to turn around or look at him or even acknowledge his presence. The second the doors slid open, she jumped out.

Then and only then did she turn back, holding the elevator door back with one hand.

"It was just stupid bedroom chitchat," she claimed. "The love thing, I mean. It wasn't true. Oh, and one more thing." She gave him a truly snarly smile. "Your month is up. I hope you enjoyed it."

She let go the door, but he caught it. "It hasn't even been a month since I met you."

"You were on an accelerated schedule." She took a few more steps backward. "Oh, and just so you know. You aren't the best I ever had. Top quarter, maybe."

His face was stunned as she sauntered off and the elevator doors closed on him.

"YOU GOT WHAT YOU DESERVED," Anna said caustically.

Stevie ignored her. "What have you got scheduled for me today? You know my motto... Let's Schedule Those Appearances With A Vengeance."

"That motto is a little too apt for me," Anna returned. "After what you did on *Chicago This Morning* yesterday."

"Why, what do you mean?" Stevie asked innocently.

"Let's see, how did you put it? 'Owen Dasher, boy reporter, who was fun for a few days, but couldn't get used to himself as a sex object.'" Anna's lips folded into a frown. "Charming, Stevie. You've got a real media war going here."

"So?" She lifted her shoulders in a shrug. "Isn't that a good thing? We're selling books like crazy. And it's not like it's hurting him, either. They've upped him to a column every day." Under her breath, she added, "A column which he uses to bash me, by the way."

"Why shouldn't he? You acted like an idiot. Fur coat. Grabbing him out of his office. Sex in an elevator!" Anna scoffed, her voice rising as she ticked off items. "What were you thinking?"

"It wasn't my proudest moment, okay?" But, man alive, was it good while it lasted. "I thought I was proving something."

"Yeah, that you can act like an idiot with the best of them."

"Anna, I told him..." She hesitated. "In the heat of the moment, I told him that I loved him. And he..." It felt like a fresh wound every time she thought about it. "He said he knew he could tame me, that I should admit it was the best sex I ever had and I would never be able to walk away from him, like he was so mighty and I was his sex slave or something, like he whipped out the big O's and I'd be addicted forever after."

"Was he?"

She blinked. "Was he what?"

"The best sex you ever had?"

"It's not like there's a big talent pool." Stevie fiddled with a branch on the tiny tree Anna had set up. "Of course he was the best. No contest."

"And do you want him back?" Anna asked quietly.

She bit her lip. "No." She could hear Anna starting to raise objections, and she held up one hand to forestall it. "Yes, okay? Yes. I want him. Back, front, whatever. I want him."

"SHE SAID SHE LOVED ME," he grumbled, staring blindly into his computer screen. "I should've told her how I felt, too, instead of that stupid, macho stuff about the best sex she ever had. What was I thinking?"

He slammed his fist into his desk, making three pens and a cup full of paper clips jump. "Damn it, anyway. How could I have screwed things up this badly? She gives me the green light, and I let her down. She hits me over the head with the green light, she even tells me she loves me, and I go all, I-told-you-so."

Of course, she had also made him the laughingstock of the newsroom, as well as something of a hero to some of the other men. No one knew exactly what happened in the elevator that day, and he sure wasn't going to tell them, but they all whispered about how long it was out of service, how Stevie had been spotted taking the stairs down from the fifth floor, and there was talk that someone saw Owen sneaking out the back door wearing a shirt that was open all the way down the front.

Yeah, she had done a spectacular number on him.

"I don't care. I still think she loved me." He pounded his fist again, getting the paper clip jar to go over the edge this time. "*Loves me.* Now how do I get her to quit going on television bad-mouthing me? And admit that she loves me."

"Um, Owen, are you talking to yourself for a reason?" T.J. asked, popping up from behind his computer, waving a sheaf of papers. "'Cause I have good news. I got her!"

"What have you got?" he asked.

"Everything." She grinned, sliding the stack under his nose. "Man, it took forever. But I got it. Her real name. Right there on top. Stephanie Blanton. Born in Nebraska, nowhere near Samoa. If you go down farther, I got her high school yearbook photo. And the picture off her employee badge when she worked for

Marsh-Penworthy & Main. The marketing firm. She handled Glam cosmetics and some other cool stuff."

Everything he needed to put an end to Stevie for good. Owen reached for the sheets, his heart sinking.

STEVIE WAS LYING on the floor in front of the tiny Christmas tree, wearing no makeup and no contacts, with her hair hastily mashed into a makeshift ponytail.

"Where did you get those clothes?" Anna demanded. "I've never seen you in anything like that."

She didn't answer. She was wearing the sweater and jeans Owen had bought her. She told herself she was wearing them because the temperature kept dropping and they were the only warm things she owned. It was a lie.

"Are you done with the *It's a Wonderful Life* video? Can I take it back to the video store now?"

"No," she said immediately, sitting up. "I need to watch it again."

"You've already watched it four or five times since last night." Anna shook her head. "Never mind."

In a faraway voice, Stevie lamented, "For the first time in my life, I had someone to wake up with on Christmas morning, somebody's house to go to for Christmas dinner, just like *It's a Wonderful Life*, and I blew it."

"Okay, that's it," Anna announced. "I can't take one more minute of this. I'm quitting."

That got her attention. "You're what?"

"Quitting," Anna repeated, with more spirit this time. "We started this for the right reasons, Stevie, but we got way off track. And we've long since proven that we knew this demographic like nobody else. We are so past that."

"I know."

Anna stomped out of the living room, marched into her bedroom and then marched right back. "Stevie, I'm going to try one more time, because you are my best friend, even when you're acting like a lunatic. So here goes. There is no crime in falling in love. Stop acting like you've done something horrible. And stop punishing yourself and that poor, abused man."

"I know."

But Anna was on a roll. "Go for it. Own up. Act like a big girl. Go tell him you love him. And quit acting like a horse's behind."

Stevie swung her legs around, sitting up and hugging her knees. "I can't."

"Well, whatever you do, I'm out of here." Anna looked a little sheepish as she backed toward her bedroom. "I think I'm going to Indianapolis for Christmas."

"Anna, that's wonderful!"

But she was already gone. And Stevie was once more left with her own unpleasant thoughts. "Anna," she called out. "Don't leave before I come back. I'm going out for a walk." She looked down at her outfit, at the clothes Owen had given her. "Now that I have warm clothes, I suppose I may as well use them."

She found a coat and the mittens and earmuffs he had also given her, and she set out for parts unknown. It was very odd, how she found herself tracing the path they'd walked together, mooning over the spot where they'd met the baby in the reindeer suit, gazing into the marvelous Christmas windows at Marshall Field's on State Street.

This time, when she looked into the windows, all she saw was her own strange reflection. "Who are you?" she said out loud. "Stevie? Stephanie? Or has it all melted into one crazy, mixed-up chick?"

There were no answers in the cold glass. She found herself with a sudden burning desire to go back to the skating rink. But she didn't know how to get there.

"Officer!" she called, flagging down a nearby cop. "How do I get to the skating rink? Millennium Park. Do you know where that is?"

"Turn left at the corner, walk two blocks. It'll be right in front of you," he said brusquely.

"Thank you," she offered, but he was already off, blowing his whistle at a pedestrian crossing against the light. Looked like she was on her own.

It was so cold out again today that she raced the whole way. She was huffing a little, her breath a cloud in front of her, by the time she reached the park. There were hardly any skaters. "Brrr," she whispered, rubbing her arms. Her teeth were chattering again. "I don't think I've felt warm since I left his arms."

And then it started to snow, big, fluffy flakes, and it was so pure and romantic, she felt like crying. "I want him back!" she yelled, not caring who heard. "I want Owen. Right now!"

Which was the precise moment that Owen showed up.

How was that possible? If she'd known it would work, she might have tried it a long time ago.

"Thank God I found you," he said quickly, pulling her into his embrace, giving her a good, hard squeeze and making her feel warm and runny all over again. "Your real name, the whole Stephanie Blanton thing, it's out. I tried to stop it, but my paper is running with it. Once the truth is out, the Stevie Bliss gig is over, although I suppose you could take a different angle. You know, 'You, too, can do Tae Bo and turn yourself into someone completely different....'"

"Owen, stop. Wait. I don't care." She squinted at him. "How did you recognize me? I'm not wearing any of the Stevie getup. I don't even have the blue eyes you loved."

"Oh. I didn't notice."

He didn't notice? He didn't notice. She began to feel the first stirrings of hope. He didn't notice!

"I admit," he went on, "at first, I was attracted to the curves and the legs and the whole vixen package. And I know you think I wanted to change you into someone else, less vixenish, but I really didn't care about the outside package then. It was you—the real you, I mean—that I fell in love with."

"Love?" she echoed.

"Yes." His eyes were soft and wistful. "I should've said it earlier. I love you. You gave me a gift when you said you loved me—"

"Yeah, but that's okay, because I said it under the most ridiculous circumstances, and I embarrassed you at your office and I don't know how you can ever forgive me—"

He stopped the flood of words in the smartest possible way. He kissed her.

Stevie held on tight, enjoying every warm, wonderful second of his lips on hers. "I-I didn't think you would even recognize me this way. Out of the Stevie Bliss package."

"I could spot you naked in a blizzard," he murmured, sliding his lips down her neck. He paused.

"Well, of course I could spot you naked in a blizzard..."

"Shut up and kiss me," she said breathlessly, as the snow began to fall harder. "If you want her, I think Stephanie Blanton may be available. For more than a month."

"She'd better be. She'd better not be parceling out her months to strange guys ever again." Dusted by snowflakes, he held her close. "Merry Christmas, Stephanie. It's nice to finally meet you."

"Just so you know, there never were any strange guys on a monthly basis," she said delicately. "I made that up."

"I know."

"And on second thought, you'd better call me Stevie." She shrugged. "I think somewhere along the line, I became both of them."

"I know that, too." He grinned. "Once you've had Bliss, there's no going back."

_____Epilogue_____

Christmas morning, one year later

"MERRY CHRISTMAS, STEVIE," Owen whispered, nuzzling her hair.

Not really willing to wake up and leave the warm bed just yet, she nestled closer, enjoying the sound of Owen's steady heartbeat right under her ear. With the winter wind whistling at the windows, it felt chilly in their bedroom, but as long as she pressed close to him, she was toasty.

"Time to get up and get ready for Christmas with the Dashers," he said, kissing her on the forehead.

Christmas with the Dashers... Ah, yes. Stevie smiled drowsily. She'd now experienced one Christmas, one New Year's, one Easter, one Fourth of July, one Labor Day, one Halloween and one Thanksgiving with his rambunctious clan. They were all great, but Christmas... Last year's Christmas at his mother's house had been a real eye-opener. So many presents, so much food, so many people, all crammed into one small home, with his beaming mom in the center of the action. It was everything Stevie had dreamed of, like every sappy Christmas movie she'd ever seen rolled into one.

"Stevie? Are you awake?" Owen slid to a sitting position, his back against the rounded headboard of their new sleigh bed, dragging her up with him. "C'mon kid. Time to open those beautiful brown eyes."

"They're hazel," she mumbled, opening her eyes enough to send him a grumpy look.

Owen grinned. "I knew that would wake you up."

But she held on, circling her arms around his chest. "It can't be time to get up. The alarm hasn't gone off yet."

She had no sooner spoken than the darned thing clicked and began to sing on the bedside table. Set to the radio, it blared out "Santa Claus is Coming to Town," perfectly selected just to mock her.

Stevie shoved her head under the pillow. "Not that song again."

"Aw, come on," Owen teased, poking around the covers, slipping one hand inside her flannel pajamas to tickle and tease her. "I have good memories of that song playing in a certain elevator with a certain lady wearing nothing but a little scrap of silk and an Open Me First tag."

"That was no lady. That was your wife," she said breathlessly, trying to bat his hands away. Instead, she ended up on her back, with her pajama buttons all undone and Owen's hands roving all sorts of places.

His expression was positively wicked, and he bent to kiss her more fully, now fooling with the drawstring at the top of her pajama pants. After loosening the garment, he traced one finger all the way from her chin to her belly button, snaking that finger onto dangerous turf. "So, wife, how come every time I strip you out of these damn things they end up back on again?"

"I love you stripping me out of them," she said

sweetly, turning onto her side so she could reach for him, too. She never got enough of his skin under her hands. "Careful, though. If we play hide the pajamas one more time this morning, we may never get up." She sighed extravagantly. "Just think. We could make love for hours and totally skip going to Lora's for Christmas."

"You're making it sound very attractive, I have to admit." But after one more long kiss, Owen pulled away.

"Owen! You can't stop now."

"Don't have any choice. Believe me, I'd rather unwrap you than any presents, but..." He smiled, that beautiful, megawatt smile that made every nerve ending in her body hum to life. "But people are expecting us." More lightly, dropping a kiss on her nose, he added, "My mom will give us hell if we're late. And the kids will kill us if they have to wait till noon to open their presents."

"Think I've been nice enough this year to get something good?" she inquired, offering a saucy smile. "No, wait, I've been very, very naughty, and I already got something very, very good." She made a grab for him just as he tossed back the covers and jumped out of bed on his side. He stood there for a moment, grinning at her, and she gazed at him with a sort of awe.

He's all mine. How did I get so lucky?

Meanwhile, she still hadn't figured out how he managed to sleep in the buff and generate enough heat for a furnace while she wore flannel pajamas and froze to death the moment he left the bed. As she rebuttoned her pajama top and contemplated that question, he padded around the bed on his way to the master bath, giving her a glorious view. Stark naked, all man, blatantly aroused, he took her breath away. Never failed.

"Are you sure we can't be a little late to your sister's?" she asked hopefully.

"C'mon. I'll run the shower, get it good and hot, and then we can share." He quirked his head in the direction of the bathroom. "Moving was worth it just for the double shower."

"I'll say," she murmured. They'd only been in their beautiful new graystone, a restored three-flat turned into one house, for a few months, and already that luxurious bathroom had paid for itself.

Of course, the new place was also worth it in terms of distance from his sister. Now they could be as noisy or exuberant as they wanted without fear of tipping off Lora or her kids to just exactly what mischief was going on upstairs.

As she listened to the sound of waters rushing in the shower, Stevie snuggled back into the covers, considering how far she and Owen had come since their first Christmas morning a year ago. Although it seemed as if everything in her life had changed, one thing had not. Against all odds, *Blissfully Single* was still on the bestseller lists, still generating royalties for her and Anna, even without a media creation like Stevie Bliss on the frontlines to fan the flames.

The money she continued to make from the book had partially funded the new house, and she hoped she could use it to launch a new business venture, too. Stevie sat up, biting her lip as Owen stepped back into the bedroom, a towel wrapped around his waist. Steam trailed behind him from the open door.

"Coming?" he asked.

"Owen, there's something I need to tell you." She

wasn't sure how to broach this. "I want to do it now, before we get caught up in the Christmas rush at your sister's house, with all the kids and the packages and hoopdedoo."

"Can you tell me in the shower?"

"No. Not really. Because then you'll be naked and I'll be naked and I won't be able to concentrate. Better do it now." She gazed at him, trying to gauge his reaction.

He'd weathered so many storms over her, with criticism of his columns and his methods and his journalistic ethics. Okay, so the end result was that he now had a nationally syndicated column and a very nice book deal of his own. But Stevie had lain low ever since the whole unraveling of her public persona before Christmas last year, and he had shielded her every step of the way.

So far, Owen hadn't suggested even once that she should re-enter the public arena. He seemed content that she stay put where she was, off-limits, under wraps, nothing more than Owen's girlfriend and now wife, refusing to discuss or explain what had happened to Stevie Bliss. They'd managed to make their summer wedding as beautifully discreet and quiet as the rest of their lives, with no press and no public statements about how the *Blissfully Single* poster girl had made the transition to Blissfully Married without so much as a backward glance. But if she opened up her life again, if she took on this new proposition... How would Owen handle that?

"What is it?" he asked, crossing back to sit on the bed beside her. "Is it Lora? I know you don't want to go to her place for Christmas, but trust me, it will be okay."

"It's not that," she tried.

But Owen went on, "I know you think she hates you, but I'm telling you, she's really warming up. It's supposed to be a surprise, but she and the girls made you a Christmas jumper, just like the ones they wear. It'll be waiting for you under the tree. So see? She must like you."

That made Stevie laugh out loud, getting her off track. "You're kidding, right? The famous red corduroy Christmas jumpers? I'm not sure I'm the type."

"Well, you can be." He took hold of her by the lapels of her pajamas. "Red flannel pj's with reindeer all over them are sort of in the same ballpark."

She reached up to give him a sweet, lingering kiss, leaving her hands framing his face. "Owen, you are incredibly adorable, as usual, and I appreciate that you're worried I don't like your sister, but I'm past that. Really. And your mom and your other sisters are great."

"They love you, Stevie. And so do I," he said softly. "More than I can even believe sometimes."

Her heart seemed to swell with the rightness and joy of this moment, of every moment since she'd fallen in love with Owen. "I love you so much. You're the best thing that ever happened to me."

And here she was, off track again.

"Owen," she began again, determined to get it right this time. "You're wonderful. Your whole family's wonderful. Believe me, this is nothing to do with any of them." She paused. "It's about me."

"What about you?" He gave her a measuring glance. "Are you sorry you finally agreed to get married? I know it was a tough one for you, but I really think—"

She placed a finger against his lips. "Owen, I am *so* not sorry we got married. Don't even think that. You know I'm crazy about you and our new house and every minute we're together, it just gets better and better. Every single minute."

"Then what?"

"It's me," she said again, rising from the bed, turning back, still not sure how to put it properly. Finally, she just came out with it. "I've spent this whole last year hiding out. And while hiding out with you is pretty spectacular, I've been thinking..."

"Ah." He nodded. "I wondered when you'd start itching to get back into the real world."

"Really? So it's okay with you?" She leapt into his lap, knocking him backward into the bed. "I have this great idea, Owen. Better than *Blissfully Single*. I mean, I have oodles of money, and I miss working with Anna, and I've always wanted to be in marketing, always. That's how *Blissfully Single* got started, you know. So I was thinking what can I do with money and with Anna that involves marketing? I have this idea that Anna and I can launch our own firm, better than Marsh-Penworthy ever had a hope of being—"

"Slow down, slow down," Owen interrupted, trying to sit up. "A marketing firm? Not another book? I thought you might want to write *Blissfully Married* or something."

"No. Why would I want to write it? I'm already living it," she said hastily. "Besides, I think I'm out of the book game. But if Anna and I had our own firm—"

"You could be like Lucy and Ethel and get into all kinds of crazy scrapes," he said wryly.

"No, no. More like Bette Midler and Barbara Hershey in *Beaches*, except Barbara Hershey dies, which is not what I'm going for—"

"Be quiet," Owen said, covering her mouth with his own as he stood up and then swung her swiftly into his arms. With a determined look on his gorgeous face, he carried her off toward the bathroom. "The idea is great. I think you'll be fabulous. And I don't want to run out of hot water while you debate what movie it's like."

Stevie held on tight, trying not to bounce up and down. "You really think this sounds okay? I'll have to be out there, you know, talking to people, making connections, trying to scare up some clients. My chickens may very well come home to roost."

Inside the bathroom, Owen dropped her, reaching around her to open the shower door. "Hon, as long as your chickens come home to me," he muttered, concentrating on unhooking her buttons one more time, "I don't mind a little roosting."

"It may get ugly."

"You can handle it." He stepped back into the shower, holding out his hand. "We can handle it together."

Together. The magic word.

As long as she was with Owen, *together* had the most amazing sound.

"How did I get so lucky?" Her lips curved into a happy smile as she slid out of her clothes and edged into the shower, up against the slick, wet, warm body of the man she loved. Tangling her arms around his neck, she whispered, "Merry Christmas, Owen."

$ Saving Money $ Has Never Been This Easy!

Just fill out and send in this form from any October, November and December 2002 books and we will send you a coupon booklet worth a total savings of $20.00 off future purchases of Harlequin and Silhouette books in 2003.

Yes! It's that easy!

I accept your incredible offer!
Please send me a coupon booklet:

Name (PLEASE PRINT)

Address   Apt. #

City   State/Prov.   Zip/Postal Code

In a typical month, how many
Harlequin and Silhouette novels do you read?

❏ 0-2   ❏ 3+

097KJKDNC7   097KJKDNDP

Please send this form to:
   In the U.S.: Harlequin Books, P.O. Box 9071, Buffalo, NY 14269-9071
   In Canada: Harlequin Books, P.O. Box 609, Fort Erie, Ontario L2A 5X3

Allow 4-6 weeks for delivery. Limit one coupon booklet per household. Must be postmarked no later than January 15, 2003.

HARLEQUIN®
Makes any time special ®

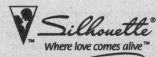

Silhouette®
Where love comes alive™

If you enjoyed what you just read,
then we've got an offer you can't resist!

Take 2 bestselling
love stories FREE!
Plus get a FREE surprise gift!

eHARLEQUIN.com

community | membership
buy books | authors | online reads | magazine | learn to write

buy books

♥ We have your favorite books from Harlequin, Silhouette, MIRA and Steeple Hill, plus bestselling authors in Other Romances. Discover savings, find new releases and fall in love with past classics all over again!

online reads

♥ Read daily and weekly chapters from Internet-exclusive serials, and decide what should happen next in great interactive stories!

magazine

♥ Learn how to spice up your love life, play fun games and quizzes, read about celebrities, travel, beauty and so much more.

authors

♥ Select from over 300 Harlequin author profiles and read interviews with your favorite bestselling authors!

community

♥ Share your passion for love, life and romance novels in our online message boards!

learn to write

♥ All the tips and tools you need to craft the perfect novel, including our special romance novel critique service.

membership

♥ FREE! Be the first to hear about all your favorite themes, authors and series and be part of exciting contests, exclusive promotions, special deals and online events.

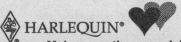

HARLEQUIN®

Makes any time special®—online...

Visit us at
www.eHarlequin.com

HARLEQUIN® *Blaze*™

From:	Erin Thatcher
To:	Samantha Tyler; Tess Norton
Subject:	Men To Do

Men To do!

Ladies, I'm talking about a hot fling with the type of man no girl in her right mind would settle down with. You know, a man to *do* before we say "I do." What do you think? Couldn't we use an uncomplicated sexfest? Why let men corner the market on fun when we girls have the same urges and needs? I've already picked mine out....